DARKHORSE'S

Get the FREE short story prequel to the Amsterdam Afterlife Series from MaryVanAmsterdam.com

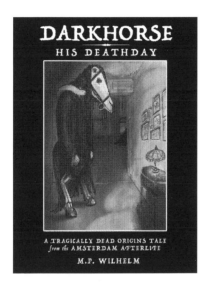

CONTINUE THE JOURNEY W/ BOOK TWO

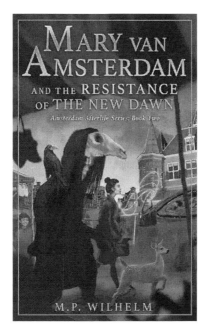

Amsterdam Afterlife Series: Book Two

MARY VAN AMSTERDAM AND THE TRAGICALLY DEAD IN RECOVERY

AMSTERDAM AFTERLIFE SERIES: BOOK ONE

M. P. WILHELM

"I must uphold my ideals, for perhaps the time will come when I shall be able to carry them out."
- Anne Frank

~

Mary van Amsterdam: Guardian of the Tragically Dead in Recovery in the Amsterdam Afterlife

~

www.MaryVanAmsterdam.com

1

Nestled together in the tallest house on the canal, the Tragically Dead in Recovery were never safer, or better cared for, than by their dedicated guardian, Mary van Amsterdam.

As the sky dimmed, stars emerged through the massive windows in the attic ceiling. It had been a hectic afternoon of back-to-back sessions. Despite her tireless dedication, Mary faced fierce resistance from an intimately familiar horse spirit.

Helping a tormented soul to come to terms with their death is a process that requires the cooperation of the individual. On this night, Darkhorse was anything but cooperative.

His corporeal form took on that of a hollow skeleton—an assemblage of dusty equine bones, capped by a large, sunbleached skull. He towered in the armchair across from Mary, under a black, hooded cloak—a silky sweep of dark mane fell to the side, obscuring half his face, to reveal but one of his empty eye sockets.

Despite his macabre appearance and somber demeanor, Mary knew Darkhorse was a shy and gentle soul. She'd treated him ever since her arrival decades ago. Cherishing him, both as his guardian, and a companion, she would never neglect her dearest, dead horse friend.

Darkhorse remained elusive—his answers were curt. He avoided eye contact, and his long pale skull peered either just over Mary's shoulder or off to the side.

Tired as she was, Mary couldn't be blamed if she postponed the session, dismissing the ambivalent spirit, to spend some much needed time alone. She could run herself a hot bath and escape into a book. But her work with the dead was her calling.

Mary swept an index finger, the pendant on her necklace glowed, and the rotund teapot that was resting, lifted and sailed through the air toward her. It tilted, filled the cup, then returned upright, hovering in place for a moment.

Mary swept her index finger, moving a rotund teapot through the air, tilting to fill a hovering cup.

"More tea?" she asked.

"No, thanks," his deep voice moaned. Again, his attention seemed drawn to a far corner of the room.

Mary suspected that this dodgy exhibition revealed a setback from the independence he'd achieved in recent years. She knew his troubled inner world well. It was a morass dominated by lonely regrets, profound despair, and a strong undercurrent of insecurity. To complicate matters, he'd unconsciously set up an array of emotional traps rife for self-sabotage. She was certain now, that something substantial was keeping him from engaging that night.

After a long silence, Darkhorse blurted out, "I had lunch with Gerald. He says you agree he's ready for graduation."

The disdain in his voice took Mary aback.

There it was.

Mary paused, avoiding the cliché, "How does that make you feel?" response. Instead, she drew a soft breath. She tilted her head to encourage him to continue without overt prompting.

"I am happy for him, of course," he added, to soften his statement.

"Gerald is a good friend. You should be glad for him." Mary looked for his reply as she took a sip from her tea.

Darkhorse continued, "I guess. The last few graduations embarrassed me. I've been here longer than every graduate including Gerald. They all move on while I stay stuck here. I'm not getting any better. I'm not anywhere near that rhino's level, and I think I work much harder than him to get through each day. I'm tired of always feeling so ashamed. I'm sick of being sick."

It was true. Gerald had developed an enviable state of enlightenment. He was by far the most advanced among the Tragically Dead in Recovery. He meditated by the canal each dawn, and took on other practices, that seemed to have endowed him with an exceptional level of patience and mindfulness. Even with the most challenging housemates, he

3

remained consistently gracious. There was no question the rhino was ready to move on to the next phase of existence, and it made sense that Darkhorse would be envious.

Darkhorse struggled every day since he arrived and he had been in the afterlife many times longer than Gerald.

"I'll never be like Gerald. I'm a mess."

"Be careful with your negative self-talk. You're making great strides considering the pain you've endured. Your tragic death is unique to you. So too, is your path to recovery. Everyone heals at their own pace. No good can come from comparing your journey to others with envy." Mary again took a sip of tea hoping Darkhorse was processing her advice. He was looking down, tapping together the tips of his waxy front hooves. He peered up in apparent desperation, and his voice cracked, "Tomorrow is the day, y'know?" he said.

"Yes, I know. Have you been using the coping strategies?"

"*Ja*, trying, but sometimes I just can't concentrate. I always get distracted and lose my focus."

"That's all right. It's part of the process too. When you slip out of it, don't let it stop you. Acknowledge it and refocus."

"Late into the night, I still lie awake. My mind grinds in circles, hung-up on the same things."

"What things are you focusing on? Do you continue to fixate on the icy bridge?" Darkhorse kept quiet. "Or fearing the recurring affliction when you wake up?" she asked.

"The morning curse definitely still sucks, but it's not what I obsess on as much as overall regret. I can't believe how naïve I was. I was so proud of myself—such a great and noble fire horse," he said with self loathing sarcasm. "I thought I was this great hero, but I wound up killing more Amsterdammers than I saved. When I am home, unless I am triggered, I'm most regretful about my life overall. But when I see that bridge I can't avoid thinking about it."

"This is good!" she said.

"How?" he said incredulously.

"You are no longer obsessing with the minutiae of the accident. It's a sign that you are broadening your perspective and dealing with the consequences of life and death more objectively. It means you are developing a healthier, more detached perspective on your past. This is a meaningful sign of progress!" Mary sat upright. "A reason to celebrate!"

Darkhorse stared ahead, expressionless. Mary saw that he didn't share her optimism. She subdued her enthusiasm and leaned forward to reconnect with him.

"Darkhorse, be patient with yourself. You earned this time in the afterlife, so keep at it. You are doing it on your own terms and at your own pace. Rather than getting sent back, it has afforded you this time to reflect on your life, and your death, so you may recover from the trauma. I'll tell you, my dear friend..." Mary set down her tea and fell back into the oversized chair, "There are aspects of this construct that will always be mysterious. Many of the afterlife mechanisms remain a mystery, but I know this: You will find peace if you don't give up."

Mary hoped Darkhorse would acknowledge his progress and accept a morsel of her encouragement.

He looked up. "What about Fawn? Gerald doesn't seem to care about her feelings at all. It's gonna break her heart when she hears he's leaving," he said.

"Don't worry about Gerald and Fawn right now. Let's get back to you. How are you going to handle tomorrow?"

"I don't know." Darkhorse sat still, then looked down again.

"I need you to open up again to make progress. How do you feel about tomorrow?"

"I... to be honest, this morning," his voice cracked, "every morning for the past few weeks, I've barely even made it to the Key House."

"Oh? Why didn't you tell me sooner?"

Darkhorse whimpered, his voice quivering. He lifted his front hooves to his face. "I'm too embarrassed. I didn't want to tell you."

His sorrow turned to frustration.

"I think I need you to go with me. Tomorrow is my Death-day. You can't leave me to go alone again. Be there for me, as my best friend, I'm begging you!" He was spiraling. "I hoped I would get better on my own, but my flashbacks and blackouts have returned. I get them on *Berenbrug* every time now. It's terri-fying, Mary! Then, when I come to, and someone is asking me if everything is all right, I am either petrified or so mad I want to shove them into the canal. I hate nosey people—especially tourists."

The old horse's spirit cried, his tears tinting the porous lower rim of his eye socket a shade darker. Mary too welled up with tears. Poor Darkhorse must have been hiding terrible pain. Despite her weekly sessions and intuitive powers, she somehow hadn't noticed. This was a pattern she knew well.

As the church bells rang out from *Westertoren* (the Tower of the West Church), tissues floated across from the table, making a brief stop in front of each of them.

"Since it is my Deathday tomorrow, will you go with me? Promise you'll help me," Darkhorse pleaded.

Mary was reluctant because she wanted him to be self-reliant. Last year on his Deathday, she hadn't had to escort him. But the sweet morose soul needed her, both as a friend and a guardian. His Deathday was historically the worst day of the year, but once he got past it, the day after found him at his best. Still, perhaps they could capitalize on that upward momentum after bottoming out. If he could just get through tomorrow. He tilted his head down in sorrow, in the way she couldn't resist.

"*Oké*, I will go with you," she agreed. "I will see you get there, my sweet friend."

"Oh, thank you, Mary. I am sorry to be such a burden to you."

"You are no burden, my darling. We are done for tonight. I need to get to sleep, so I may be at my best for you tomorrow."

Mary smiled and stretched her arms above her raven bun, untucked her pallid, bare feet from under her, and took a step onto the soft rug. With arms outstretched, she approached, placing one hand around his boney ribcage, as her other brushed his mane away from the front of his eye sockets. He rested his skull on her shoulder, and she pressed her head against his. Tears dripped off his face and wetted her cheek.

"Thank you, Mary."

She stepped back and smiled in her caring way, wiping the tears from his skull. "See you in the morning," she whispered.

Leaving the door to the attic suite open, Darkhorse, clopped down the steep wooden stairs to retreat to his private bedroom.

Mary took a long blink and a deep breath. Looking over her notes as she walked to the door. As she extended her arm into the hall to take handle, a sudden fluttering mass emerged from the darkness.

It was Hans, a graylag goose. He landed with a thump at the top of the stairs, stood up, and charged past her through the doorway.

"Mary, we have to do something about the gambling."

"Again?" Mary said exasperated.

"Yes, the birds invented a new card game and are fleecing the mice," he said. "They are turning the mantel into a darn casino, I tell you! In just three nights, they've hoarded all of this month's ice-cream tokens for themselves."

"Okay, I'll talk to them tomorrow. The silly mice also need to learn their lesson, they never win! Oh, Hans, it's been a long day."

"That's all right, Mary, I just wanted you to know."

Mary looked up and saw that the goose had a spectral echo of the bottle-cap ring that ensnared and killed him.

"Hans darling, you have a manifestation of that plastic ring again. Let me get it off you."

"Oh, yes, I hardly noticed. It develops whenever I get worked up."

The goose stood still and with a click of her finger, Mary dissolved the ring into a wispy trail of blue smoke.

"Thank you, Mary," said the goose as he departed.

She finished, organized, and filed her session notes, prepared for bed, and slid into her refreshing, crisp sheets and cracked the book she was reading. She hoped she could get through at least one chapter before she dozed off.

She almost succeeded, but after about five minutes of rereading the same page, she had to accept that she couldn't focus.

Mary set the novel down and removed her necklace. Holding it in her left hand and with a flick of her finger, the reading light turned off. She placed the pendant and chain on her nightstand.

Sounds and chatter from the floors below subsided, and just as she was about to doze off, Mary heard the windows open as the nocturnal members of the Tragically Dead departed for the night. Gazing through her enormous overhead skylight, she watched the silhouettes of the dead bats flutter off into the moonlit sky.

The growing mayhem at the house and the new troubles with Darkhorse concerned her. Something about his recent relapse into fragility reminded her of poor Peter, her childhood companion from her time in the living realm. When she'd outgrown him, she thought the best thing to do was to abruptly and unceremoniously let Peter go. But she could never do that to one of her Tragically Dead. Mary looked forward to helping Darkhorse in the morning.

2

A glowing green orb raced through the early morning air. It pulsed, whizzing through the moonlit system of canals and squares at a time of night when only the most fortified ventured out into central Amsterdam.

The brilliant sphere banked high around the corner of *Herengracht* then veered down close to the undulating surface. Its luminance reflected off the silvery channel as it moved closer to the water and pulled up a fine spray as it zoomed along. It soared under a small bridge, then rose, ascending through trees and over the brick-paved road and whisked past windows. Finally, the orb reached the tops of the houses and wove through the series of hooks, gables, and spires, darting lively over rooftop crests toward its destination.

The glowing sphere jostled to a stop over Mary's house. Standing greater than its neighbors, the tall, narrow house featured enormous windows on its angled roof with three vast skylights.

The orb descended, sinking without resistance through the shingles, wood frame, and plaster. It slowed to a stop, resting directly above its target. It was seeking the "Guardian of the Tragically Dead in Recovery," Mary van Amsterdam.

With the souls of these innocent friends nestled safely throughout the floors beneath her, Mary was active in a recurring dream, helping untangle an unsolvable abstract obstacle. A deep pulsing sound broke through her state. The noise wasn't unpleasant, but as designed, it shook her just enough to rouse her toward alertness.

Mary opened her eyes to see the illuminated object hovering there. On the foggy edge of sleep, she pushed her hair away from her face and attempted to recover consciousness. The messenger orb pulsed green and white, showing the information was of standard importance. With a wave of her hand, the device presented its message. Projected from the sphere was the moving image of her fellow "Guardian of the Studious Dead in Research" in Prague. She knew Jerome well, always appreciating his wit and kind disposition.

"Dearest Mary," he said solemnly, "we kindly request your presence at the tower at Týn. We have recovered a soul in dire need of your gifts. It's a case of fog and cool rain. Please come at once."

A thin light beam cast from the sphere across the room to Mary's notebook. The glowing information stream swept rapidly, transmitting details about the spirit to which she was to tend.

She stretched out while rolling over on her hip toward the side of the bed and retrieved her necklace from her nightstand. The pendant's etched symbols were but one sign of its many secrets—some unknown even to her. The cold metal came to life in her warm hand and glowed a faint azure through the gaps between her fingers.

She gestured with a graceful motion toward her notebook. It lifted itself above her desk, hovered out of her office, passed through opened pocket doors, and breezed straight over to her bed. She took it from the air and quickly skimmed the brief.

"Oh, the poor thing. Well, I guess that's all the sleep I get tonight."

Mary sighed and gestured to the orb to record her reply. It turned orange and recorded her words. The amber glow pulsed with each syllable:

"Thank you, Jerome. I will leave at once." She swiped her hand to the left and pinched her fingers. The object resumed a green radiance and shot up, passing back through the ceiling, before speeding off into the night.

The early hour put a cold pit in Mary's stomach. Her discomfort compounded, remembering that she'd promised Darkhorse she would walk him to the Key House. Disheartened by the dreadful scheduling conflict, she collapsed onto the bed, wishing she could crawl back under the warm covers and never come out. As much as she loved Darkhorse, her dedication to easing the suffering of a freshly arrived Tragically Dead spirit outweighed the need to tend to his recent shortfall. It was her highest duty to heed the summons of a fellow guardian to receive and orient a new arrival.

Aal should be able to escort Darkhorse in the morning. The train route would take all day, and spirits don't fly on airplanes so she couldn't both accompany her dead horse friend and reach Prague before dusk. However, she hoped there was some way. Mary always kept the afterlife rail schedule in her black handbag.

To the casual observer, Mary's handbag was a mere fashion accessory. But inside, it was remarkably vast with impossible space for accommodating any size of Tragically Dead soul. It had her entire assortment of potions, and more books than a wheelbarrow could manage. From an outside pocket, the thin, Afterlife International Railway timetable emerged and hovered across the room.

The paper crackled as the seams expanded, suspending in the air before her. Mary located the departure times for trains traveling from Amsterdam to Prague Central Station, reading as she stood. Her pendant glowed brighter in her hand as it emitted meandering streams of blue light. The tendrils wrapped around her body and lifted her off the ground. The broad creased page rose along with her to keep level with her sightline as she read. Her black dress glided down over her raised arms, briefly disrupting her examination of the timetable. Simultaneously, leggings rolled up her legs and compressed right into place as her eyes scanned for the best route to Prague.

With the collar on her shoulders, Mary held the necklace in her lips. Feeling that she should get a move on, she fastened the dress's top button behind her neck by hand, while her belt wrapped around and secured itself on her waist. She took her pendant out of her mouth and drew the strand over her head, and the enchanted glowing amulet came to rest over her heart.

The schedule confirmed that Mary would have to leave for the station immediately to arrive in Prague by sunset. She wouldn't be able to keep her promise to Darkhorse. Frustrated, she noted the route number and departure time to herself. With a dismissive wave, the paper folded itself and returned to its place in the bag.

Black shoes fit themselves onto her feet, latching just right as she tied her hair into a high bun. In less than a minute, she dressed and was ready to depart. Mary silently glided out of the attic suite, hovering a hand's width above the steps as her purse floated, following behind. With glowing cerulean blue eyes, similar to the glow of the talisman around her neck, she peered into the depths of the darkest rooms. As she drifted through the empty halls, her passing created subtle wind drafts that only disturbed the corners of tablecloths and curtains.

She found each of her beloved, tranquil spirit friends assembled in clusters sleeping throughout the house.

Fireplace embers maintained a warm glow in the large, main room. The assembly of snoozing birds always sat before it as if perpetually cold. They'd frozen to death distant winters ago, after escaping their neglectful owners and perished in the elements. The traumatized avian souls huddled close, snoring, eyes closed, and feathers fluffed. Next to them, a semicircle of mice reclined in tiny toy furniture, some bundled in napkins.

A row of mid-sized species rested further out from the fire. These were the unlikeliest of bedfellows. Suffering together in the afterlife, predators cuddled peacefully with prey.

In the corner near the window, a young doe snoozed beneath a blue baby blanket draped over the rotund belly of a rhinoceros. The rhino was Gerald, who Darkhorse lamented was ready for graduation, but Mary was equally proud of both.

From down the hall, tonal snores reverberated. They came from in the private bedroom, emitted by the hollow skull of Darkhorse. Mary knew he needed his sleep to face tomorrow. Recalling his desperate pleas, and her promise to accompany him, left her feeling guilty. She raised her fingers, blessing him as she passed his room.

Her troubled but beloved friends were all in place as she continued out of the tall canal-house.

Mary secured the front door and stepped from her cold cement stoop. The streetlights illuminated her grim form as she hurried along the brick pavement lining the glossy canals toward Amsterdam's central station.

In the distance, a fuzzy-looking group of living narrowly dodged a tram. Mary hoped to avoid the rowdy crew scampering in her direction, and crossed to the far side of the canal, even though it was slightly less direct.

In the afterlife it was the living who were the apparitions. Their partially opaque form was barely visible. At this hour, there were usually revelers wandering around the canal district —tourists mostly, stalking about inebriated by substance and/or jetlag.

In extreme states of intoxication, living souls could garner views into the spirit realm. If they realized they saw a ghost, it inevitably led to unwanted gawking or uncontrollable screaming. If not scared off, they would bombard a soul with the predictably mundane string of questions. She had no patience for this now.

Opposite the waterway from Mary, the drunken gang of barely conscious humans staggered along. Each wore matching custom tee-shirts, and they swayed as they sang off-key, arms over each other's shoulders. The one in the center donned a paper crown, and after a hard blink in Mary's direction, clumsily halted the group. Her face crinkled as she sensed they had spotted her.

The glimpse of her semi-transparent form seemed to captivate him, and he leaned heavily on a friend and pointed across the canal to Mary.

"Oi, look at her!" he implored in a high, cracking voice.

She heard the muffled slurry outburst through the cross-dimensional membrane and rolled her eyes. Maintaining her stride, Mary was determined to intercept Aal before reaching the station. But now, every member of the raucous crew had glimpsed her paranormal form. Intrigued, they gingerly approached the edge to get a better look at her specter across the channel. Each swig from the shared bottle unwittingly sharpened a more detailed view of her ghostly silhouette. Another called out something crude.

Fed up, Mary tapped her talisman and as it glowed blue. Mary faced them from the other side of the canal. Her eyes blazed a solid flash of cerulean illumination as her spectral form lunged menacingly at them. For extra effect, she conjured fangs framed within a demented smile. In an instant, she appeared to vanish entirely into a thin wisp of vapor.

The group unleashed astonished expletives, and the startled proto-groom leaned forward with his foot caught under the tire barrier. It was there to prevent parking vehicles from accidentally rolling off of the steep precipice, but useless to keep him from meeting such a fate. A groomsman reached out, only clasping the paper crown, holding out the torn thing in vain as he splashed into the frigid channel. Just another raucous predawn event in Amsterdam—drunk tourists seeing ghosts, falling into canals.

The houses on the east side of the water glowed golden as the sun rose, and Mary continued along the grand canal at a solid clip. She expected the distinct frequency of her footsteps on the cobblestone to rouse the attention of her well-attuned friend if he was coursing below the murky waters.

Sure enough, as she approached *Brouwersgracht*, something in the water splashed. Aal, the ancient and mystical eel, was Mary's longtime mentor in the afterlife. His head popped out of the channel and he exclaimed, "Where are you off to at this hour, dear Mary?"

"I'm headed to Prague for some fog and cool rain. Would you mind letting the house know? Please also tell Darkhorse that I absolutely had to break my plans with him, on account of duty. I am heartbroken because in session last evening, I promised to accompany him today."

"I will," assured the eel.

"He is in such a fragile state, and it is his Deathday. I hope he forgives me."

"I'm sure he'll understand. Not to worry. I'll ensure he gets there safely."

Mary continued walking to the station as Aal swam alongside.

"Fog and cool rain, eh? It's a great honor to receive only the souls most in need of our support. It will be nice to have another feathered friend among us," he said. Her eel mentor always had a way of putting things into the proper perspective.

"And he is a raven!" she said gleefully.

"Fantastic! Well, Prague is also delightful this time of year. It shouldn't be a surprise if I rendezvous with you tomorrow." The eel's grin revealed two tiny teeth, one above and below.

"That would be lovely."

"Safe travels, Mary. Bon voyage!"

Aal tossed three delicate lilies to her. As they reached her, the bloom enchantingly formed a small corsage as she caught them. With a binding spell, she affixed it just below her collarbone and soared away in haste. The kind eel's inventive gestures of friendship were tokens of solidarity that seemed always to arrive when most needed.

At the station's entrance, her ghostly form swept through faint cross-dimensional clouds of tobacco smoke from the equally hazy early morning commuters. She double-checked her track number and route information and headed to the platform. Just as she approached, Mary's custom rail car manifested, attached at the end of the living train. A dead conductor swooped in and welcomed her aboard.

She settled into her cozy cabin, hoping to catch up on her sleep. Portions of the windows on each side held spirit-glass. Reclining on the soft, comfortable seat, she turned to observe the bustling track platform. Through the enchanted panes, she watched the adjacent realm of the living. It was always interesting to study the goings-on of modern life. She enjoyed noting minor observations, such as the recent trend among Amsterdammers, to tend toward wearing larger headphones than in years past. She wondered if the sound were better, or if they showed prestige.

The train rolled out. Mary sat back with a fresh cup of tea to ease her sorrow and fatigue. As they rounded the outer east side of Amsterdam, the tracks turned southeast. Across the countryside, blurs of emerald valleys and vast modern greenhouses raced by. She fell asleep, missing the views of the old-fashioned windmills and distant village towers she usually admired. As her mind wandered off, she tried to avoid dwelling on poor Darkhorse and the taxing trials he would have to endure on his Deathday without her.

3

B ack at home, in immense pain, Darkhorse strained to reach and flick his bedroom light off, then on again, seven times. He could barely reach it with his right hoof due to the insane metal and leather bindings that connected his joints and restricted his movement. He slapped the lock knob on his chamber door up and down seven times too. Then he closed the door, locked it with the key that hung around his neck with his teeth and began the methodical descent down the steep and narrow stairway that led to the exterior door.

Still on the inside of the front door, he unlatched, latched, and again unlatched the lock before pulling it open. Expecting that Mary was on the other side, likely hearing his ritual, embarrassed him a little bit, but she understood his problems, and he simply couldn't resist the compulsion.

Darkhorse swung the door open and hunched down to fit through the narrow doorframe. Cloaked grimly, his skeletal frame leaned out, and his massive, bare equine skull emerged. The bike rack across the lane on the edge of the canal was in clear view, but there was no Mary. His head swayed left and right, and left again, peering up and down the canal, but still, no sign of her.

From behind the parked bikes, Aal launched out of the canal, over the rack, and the eel slid onto the pavement toward him.

"Darkhorse my friend, Mary has sent me to tell you she had to go to Prague to handle a case of fog and cool rain. So, I will have the honor of escorting you this fine morning."

"What?" Darkhorse shouted with incredulity.

"Oh, sorry," Aal calmly responded, "that probably doesn't mean anything to you. She had to go to Prague to rescue a dead airborne spirit whose last life, after consecutive lifetimes of trials, was taken short, and under substantially dark auspices."

"Great. She abandoned me!"

"Oh, Darkhorse, understand that Mary was summoned by another guardian. She had no choice and asked me to take her place. It would be my pleasure to escort you to the Key House, my friend."

Darkhorse took a deep breath, his fury teetering with heartache. He looked down and pressed his forehead firmly against the inside of the doorway. His bridle cracked against the back of his boney jaw, and this pulled the day's nonsensical web of straps to cut and pinch into the inside of his neck. He ignored the discomfort, speaking calmly but with pained exasperation.

"No, I don't want your help, Aal. I can handle this on my own."

"Darkhorse, my friend, please let me help you. I can ease your burden."

"No, I don't want your help. Leave me alone!" he shouted.

"All right, if you change your mind –" The eel was cut off.

"Just go back to your muck, silly old canal eel!"

Darkhorse's cruel outburst shocked himself. He started to

feel sick for speaking to his friend, the kind, wise eel, this way. He hoped that in his patient wisdom, Aal would understand Darkhorse's anger at the circumstances. The eel solemnly slid back into the murky depths of the water, leaving Darkhorse to face his pain and misery alone, as insisted.

"There is always someone else who needs Mary's help more than me." He seethed, then decided he had to gather his composure if he was going to make it to get his bindings removed. "No need to rush. I am in control. I am not pulling a heavy load. I am safe in the afterlife." His deep voice reverberated from his hollow skull, reciting the words given to him by Mary. For them to work, he had to believe and embrace them.

With full intention, he placed his left hind hoof (never his right) onto a precise spot on the periphery of the landing atop the concrete stoop. It always had to be just inside the dark-green painted railing, as far away as possible from what he saw as a slick, well-worn center, where paws, claws, and shoes had polished the concrete surface for centuries. The leather bindings creaked as he extended and planted his right foot to descend the steps, in his own precise manner. Now that he was standing on the stoop, he could pull out his heavy reins that dragged behind him so he could close the door.

As he descended the stoop, a gust of wind blew along the canal. Atop his knobby dome, his black hood fluttered, casting a dancing shadow above his vacant eye sockets. His long, ragged cloak snapped and cracked in the wind like a tattered battle flag, and clouds swirled overhead as crows cawed from the tree.

"My sorrow will someday pass—I have within me what I need to improve each day."

Lumbering upright on his hind legs, in the manner he had adopted in the afterlife, Darkhorse limped west toward the Jordaan district as tight bindings and straps restrained his movements.

A cavalcade of jittery shadow-forms whizzed by him on the small bridge named *Berenbrug*. Some on bicycles, others on sputtering motor-scooters. The frenzy of the living-realm morning rush hour flowed around him, sometimes passing straight through his form as he struggled forward. The enthusiastic optimism of the oblivious, living commuters seemed to mock Darkhorse's morose mood in the afterlife. At times he even felt the contrast of their joy mocked his suffering.

Darkhorse was a ghostly, skeletal carcass. His accident was years ago. But he winced as vivid flashes of it invaded his present mind. Hooves sliding across wet flagstone as the momentum of a massive cart pushed him from behind. He opened his eyes, snapping out of that harrowing memory, returning to the afterlife.

"What a cancerous waste," he cursed.

At times he resented having ever lived. If his ruminations

flew out of control, he easily fell into a state of hating the living realm's inhabitants—the clumsy citizens with their candle flames, the slippery canal bridge, the position of the café at the base of a sloping bridge, the cruel, unyielding weight of the steam engine, even the men who nurtured and trained him, driving him too fast over the bridge. All of it be damned!

Daily, the physical manifestations of his trauma added insult to injury. His feet ached terribly, and the range of motion the bindings allowed was so limited that it would easily induce a terrible panic of claustrophobia if he didn't remain calm while walking to his destination. He had to remain focused on his steps and his breath. He was nearly there.

With each painful step, the bindings creaked, and locks clanked, rattling and chipping away crumbs of his dry bones. A loose bit cruelly rattled between his skull and was always positioned in his jaw to hit a raw nerve with each step. As he stepped up a curb to cross the canal, an odd jolt of pain shot through him. In reaction to this he tried to extend his hoof to grab the guardrail, but his elbow pulled on a strap connected to his leg and he tripped, unable to extend his leg properly or reach his hoof to the guardrail. He lost his balance, and as he fell forward, his jaw struck the bridge's iron handrail. Pieces of jawbone shattered and fell into the canal as the rest of his bundled skeleton collapsed lifelessly onto the sidewalk. What remained of his cracked jaw now ached, as did his sharp joints that fell hard onto the pavement.

Finally, the pain eased, and he opened his eyes as he lay there, staring up at the dark sky. Spirit realm onlookers gathered, peering down at him. He suspected they were more curious than concerned. Clouds overhead finally gave up their lode and a downpour erupted. Onlookers scattered away, leaving Darkhorse to lie alone on display in the center of the sidewalk. Heavy sheets of rain pummeled him, and frigid sprays from bicycles splashed through him. For several minutes, he felt no desire to get up and his thoughts turned grim.

He made a grave decision. Lying flat on his back, at the edge of the canal, he put a front hoof on the lower rail and shimmied himself under the rail to the edge of the bridge and ducked his head under. With a hind hoof he pressed against one of the thick vertical rails and shoved so his weight teetered over the edge. As his weight shifted and he rolled over the edge, his tears mixed with rain and he fell toward the water. The long reins and cloak followed as he plummeted into the cold depths of *Prinsengracht* canal.

He was frustrated to not sink, but instead his chipped and shattered skeleton floated along the canal. He couldn't even drown his misery. Without care for what might happen next. He tried to rotate and float on his side. The bindings made it difficult to maneuver in the water. It hurt when he turned his head to gasp for air. He was most comfortable face down, with his head submerged, but then he could only inhale water. He couldn't aspirate to death – he was already dead. There in the afterlife he could only suffer.

HE ROLLED onto his back as heavy raindrops pounded him and splashed the water's surface around him. The ghosts of a few living-realm boats slid through him as he floated along, blocking the water for a few seconds. He felt utterly alone.

"Darkhorse, the Tragically Dead never walk alone." It was Aal's voice transmitting as though through the water. "You may have given up, but we haven't. Let me help you."

The thought that his friend spent the morning following him along the canal made Darkhorse feel truly cared for. He thought about how many times Mary said she loved him. He finally managed to imagine how much it pained her to not be there for him. He was overtaken with emotion. "Thank you, Aal, I'll take whatever help you can give."

He immediately felt his body emerge above the surface of the canal. His skeletal carcass carried into the air, and he was propped up next to an Amsterdammertje, the quintessential bollards that lined the city's pavements.

Aal slithered around to face him and spoke softly. "Darkhorse, I can help you to the Key House. Let's get this terrible burden off you."

Darkhorse gathered himself and with assistance from the eel, the his jawbone rematerialized, and he managed to stand up. With Aal's encouragement, he lurched his way up the pavement, along the canal. Dripping wet, he should have felt colder, but he was warmed by Aal's friendship. With his powerful magic, Aal could have easily levitated his carcass all the way to the destination, but what Darkhorse needed was just enough support to supplement his own efforts.

Plodding along the outside of *Prinsengracht*, Darkhorse and Aal reached the old familiar door under the large, weathered, wooden key sign.

"I'd be happy to join you, or I can leave you to it."

"I'll take it from here, Aal. You can go ahead and get back to your day."

The little eel smiled and nodded, then slithered across the red stone pavement and dove back into the canal.

Darkhorse pushed the door open and ducked down to fit in and tugged his heavy leather reins and dripping wet cloak in from the cobblestone.

"G' morning, Darkhorse. Be right with you, friend," said Jaap from across the shop.

"G' morning. I'm here again," Darkhorse replied, embarrassed as always.

"You're never a bother, my friend," he reassured casually but kindly.

The shop was very old and smelled of lubricant and scorched metal. Jaap finished tightening the screws on a disembodied, hovering door handle and began walking over to Darkhorse. The misty hardware glowed softly, then slowly set down behind him.

"*Oké*," Jaap said as he strode over to Darkhorse. He removed a device like a pocket light from his thick flannel shirt and clicked it on as he strolled across. When he reached Darkhorse he paused, looking puzzled.

"Did you swim here?"

"Sort of," Darkhorse replied.

"Sounds fun. Now, let's see what we have today."

The ritual had become routine over the decades. Jaap pulled over his wheeled work stool. Darkhorse, somber and expressionless, lifted his front hooves to the side, attempting to best actuate a *T*-pose. His encumbrances clanked and jangled until the chains were taught. He couldn't lift both hooves up all the way.

Jaap placed the end of the light in his mouth and began his appraisal, spinning around on the work stool, the coasters rolling over the concrete shop floor. He stood and circled him one more time, animated, moving in and out, assessing the wild, asymmetric configuration of interlocking chains and heavy bindings.

"Oh, that lock is one we haven't seen before, but it should

be no problem." He continued for a few more seconds before finally exclaiming, "Looks like three locks to cut through today, Darkhorse, and the rest should be easy."

"The keyholes blocked?"

"Yep, seems they always do. Not a problem though," Jaap assured. "First, let's get that bridle off."

With clenched teeth, the kind locksmith eventually snapped through the final segment of thick harnesses with several squeezes of leather cutters. Nothing on the dressings had prongs or holes. It was as if the bindings were custom cut, forged and bound, snugly and painfully, applied surreptitiously as Darkhorse slept each night. Light chains jingled as Jaap gently removed the metal bit from Darkhorse's dry skull. Immediately he felt relief. Over the course of half an hour, with blowtorch and diamond saw for the locks and chains, Jaap disassembled the intricate web of straps, locks, and chains.

Jaap was a gentle hero and a kind friend to Darkhorse. He was the only source of reprieve from the daily affliction. Completely freed, Darkhorse extended his hooves high up and far out from his body as he stretched. He tilted his head to each side. "That is so much better. I don't know what I would do without you."

The dead old Dutchman's face cracked as he said with a smile, "I'm happy to be able to provide you with some relief. Now, let's get those shoes replaced so you can get on with your day." Jaap quickly removed the rusty, archaic iron shoes nailed sloppily to his hooves and replaced the hind ones he walked on with modern, comfortable rubber booties. Rather than being affixed with nails, they slipped right onto the outside of this hooves.

Darkhorse thanked Jaap and made his way across the shop toward the exit. Just when he reached the door, Jaap hollered, "But hey, don't be a stranger when you get this curse removed.

Remember, you're always welcome to stop by for an afternoon beer."

Darkhorse tapped his hoof on a wooden counter in an affirmative manner and strode out onto the paved stone in front of the shop. The sun was shining, and the air felt fresh and light. Darkhorse took wide optimistic strides, allowing him to feel the wind through his mane as he continued his Deathday.

4

M ary studied the entire case file for the rescue, a raven, then read a few chapters in her book for pleasure. Anticipating a stop in Frankfurt, she closed her book and gazed out her window. The train was entering a forest. Darkhorse came to mind and guilt ran through her. She still mourned breaking her promise to him. Hopefully he would accept help from Aal.

After ruminating on the challenges of her beloved dead friends, she determined it was time for a little travel drink. She stretched, stepped out of the private cabin, and began down the car's narrow hallway lined with windows. The train was now well into the dark and dense German forest.

Peering out the window, Mary reflected on her time among the living. After a few moments, she sensed a cold presence and turned to find the ghost of a dutiful German ticket agent standing beside her.

"*Guten Tag. Ihr Bahnticket*

bitte?" greeted the tall agent casually.

Mary smiled and reached into her pocket. The demeanor of the agent transformed in deference to what Mary presented. The agent held Mary's Guardian identification card and stood, in apparent awe of the rare artifact. It was larger and thicker than a standard pass and made of a material unlike anything in the living realm. It was metallic, yet light and flexible. Crafted so ornately, it was more akin to a piece of jewelry than identification. The agent continued as if transfixed for an inordinate amount of time, relishing in the artifact's beauty, and with good reason. Mary's afterlife identification was unquestionably a work of art, but it was also a magical charm, enchanted in Edinburgh. Covered with animated shapes, the scrollwork and textures flowed and rolled as illustrated banners waved and weaved, revealing beneath them tiny charms and symbols. The mesmerizing elements fluttered and swarmed in and out of view, tinted with an iridescent spectrum like vivid mother-of-pearl. The constellations of elements orbited around the animated image of its holder, Mary van Amsterdam, whose portrait smiled out, cheekily winking to greet her examiner. Through the charm's enchantment, it reliably conveyed her benevolent nature to any viewer, fostering the deep sense of trust and reassurance befitting her upstanding character.

"*Scheisse,*" the steely agent calmly uttered, and for a split second cracked an involuntary grin.

"Excuse me?" Mary replied politely.

The initially disinterested agent resumed an air of indifference, coughed gently, and wished Mary a pleasant journey. The agent lingered there, while Mary politely continued on, leaving the agent to recover and resume patrolling the afterlife train cars.

MARY ENTERED the luxurious lounge car, finding it under capacity. A bar at the back capable of accommodating over a dozen thirsty passengers hosted merely a few. She walked toward the bar, passed empty cocktail tables, and approached the counter next to two spirits who must have arrived in the afterlife as young women like Mary.

Mary surmised they had both died in the 1920s, before Mary was even born. They wore cloche hats and sipped identical pale green cocktails. Mary eyed a handsome bottle of single-malt Scotch whisky at the bar, and the weathered bartender asked with a charming Spanish accent, "What may I serve you, miss?"

She ordered the scotch, served neat of course.

The ladies quickly revealed American accents and broad smiles, heartily introducing themselves.

"Always nice to meet another gal who's not afraid to drink like a man," one said with a grin.

Mary was put off by the sexist, old-fashioned implication of the statement, but graciously appreciated the well-intentioned instigation of conversation.

"I'm Laura, and this is my sister, Barbara."

"Pleasure to meet you. I am Mary."

"Nice to meet you, Mary. Isn't this a beautiful lounge car?" asked Barbara.

"It is very accommodating. Amazing how much nicer things are here in the afterlife," Mary said.

Laura replied, "Truly, I usually can't bear to look through spirit-glass, too depressing. I'm glad I croaked!"

The bartender laughed and gracefully presented Mary with an elegant pour of single-malt scotch, beside it a tumbler sidecar of cold water, and a small silver spoon.

"I am Luis, at your service," he said.

"Thank you, Luis," Mary said, and he spun away with gusto to check in with the patron at the end of the bar.

"How long have you been in the spirit realm, Mary?" asked Barbara.

"About seventy years," Mary said. "I died during the second world war."

Laura responded, "Oh, you are new! Welcome."

Alluding to the origin of the drink Mary had ordered, Barbara noted, "We haunted Scotland for a few years when we first arrived in the afterlife. Is that where you're from?"

"No, I am in Amsterdam now," Mary replied.

As if something fantastically delightful just occurred to her, Barbara stepped toward Mary. They were face to face while she firmly planted her hand on her sister's arm. "Wait, I know exactly who you are. You are Mary van Amsterdam, Guardian of the Traumatically Dead!"

Mary grinned sheepishly and confirmed while gently clarifying the often-misspoken title. "I am Mary van Amsterdam, Guardian of the Tragically Dead in Recovery."

Laura gushed, "What a pleasure! You must know Aal the eel?"

Mary giggled to herself and confirmed that she knew Aal well; in fact, she had just spoken to him on her way to the station.

"When you see him again, please tell him hello for us, Laura and Barbara!"

"No, Barbara and Laura, he will remember me more, I'm sure," Barbara quipped.

The sisters squabbled playfully, reminiscing and relaying the circumstances of their conversations with Aal. They'd "met at least three times, perhaps four." Once was on a cruise, and the others were while attending prominent social events.

While the scope and range of the eel's influence had lost most of its shock value, it never ceased amusing Mary. The women carried on gushing on about Aal, and Mary chuckled at the thought of her friend. Such a charismatic little eel, entertaining dead high-society with anecdotes and witty observations.

As they continued, Mary took notice of the quiet, solitary figure seated at a table to the side of the bar – his back was turned, and he wore a gray military uniform under a long dark jacket with the collar turned up. Expressionless, he took modest sips from his drink. His feet were crossed before his outstretched legs in long polished leather boots. Mary was curious as to who he was and from where he came. She did not recognize the uniform. It was certainly not Dutch or German, she knew those well. Perhaps he was from the living realm as there were no armies in the afterlife. Despite her heightened intuition in the afterlife, Mary could get little sense for who he was.

Realizing they had gone on far too long about Aal, the sisters resumed praise of Mary's afterlife endeavors. Thanking them for their kind words, Mary raised her drink for a warm toast with newfound acquaintances. The three elegant ladies clinked their glassware and took sips. The rich flavor of the Islay delighted Mary; it was full of character – peaty, robust, and perfectly balanced.

Mary shifted the focus of the discussion to the sisters. They were frequent patrons of touring and died in a rail accident. Despite their pastime being the manner of their demise, they spent their time in the afterlife traveling—always aboard afterlife trains or haunting luxury cruises in a perpetual quest to travel the afterlife globe. Both lovely in appearance, and vibrant in personality, the charismatic siblings disclosed that their other favorite pastime was flirting with the living at bars. Well, living or dead, it didn't much matter, but the challenge of winning the favor of a living soul was, apparently, more rewarding.

Mary then discreetly asked about the mysterious soldier. "Do you know who he is?"

"He's no fun," said Laura dismissively, "some sort of general from Krowston."

"Krowston? I've never heard of it."

"Now there is someone worth talking to." Barbara pointed to the figure of a handsome young man materializing into view from the living realm as he drank at the end bar near the dead soldier's table.

Laura pulled out a monocle of spirit-glass from her clutch, looking identical to the lens that Aal often wore. She ogled at a perfectly clear vision from the adjacent dimension. After handing it back and forth, the sisters eventually pressed Mary herself to gaze through. She did and observed a tall, athletic young man, wearing a white knit sweater with a sport team emblem.

With each sip of his potent beverage, the living-realm lad materialized more clearly, and the lens became less necessary – he was now nearly perfectly visible with the naked eye.

Sharing a knowing look, the ladies invited Mary to accompany them in garnering the attention of the intoxicated but handsome form from the living realm. Mary politely declined, and the two sisters stalked toward their newfound prey.

Now alone at the bar, Mary was approached by the consummate professional, Luis. He fulfilled his duty and struck up a polite conversation with Mary, delighted to find out she was a guardian. Together, they pitied the unsuspecting target of the sisters. The poor young fellow had absolutely no idea what he was in for and was in no state to handle them. Luis answered a few questions about the new afterlife territory, Krowston. She was alarmed when Luis informed her that their officially assigned guardian had been missing for several weeks. The general had just been briefed in Scotland and was returning to Krowston. For the time being, he would be their acting guardian.

With only one sip of whisky remaining in her glass, Mary was contemplating introducing herself to the general, even if he was only an "acting guardian."

Suddenly, the car's pocket doors slammed opened with a loud *whack*. Was there a malfunction? Perhaps someone was about to make a dramatic entrance? It certainly had Mary's attention. Menacingly, a thick black vapor poured in through the empty doorway and wafted into the room, slowly curling around corners and twirling around chair and table legs. The room quieted down, still with anticipation.

"What is that?" Barbara cried out in fear.

The bartender set down the bottle he was holding and grabbed his enchanted muddler. A monstrous, dark-cloaked figure gradually emerged through the smoky black mist. It wore a thick shroud with a large hood obscuring its head. Taller than the doorway, it gripped the sides with giant skeletal hands and crouched down to enter the car. Stepping in with massive clawed feet, once through the door, it raised its head to reveal a morose pale skull.

Mary knew this to be a Soul Reaper, but something wasn't quite right. The legion of disciplined agents carried out important duties. They were well respected and of high rank like guardians, but with a very different purpose. The egoless entities' role was limited to picking up, transporting and delivering souls between realms, and they rarely interacted with the dead for long, if at all.

There were several things off about this one. First, it had a strong, unusual odor as if it was decomposing. Secondly, the black sooty streams of smoke that it emitted seemed alive, moving of their own intention. Finally, the thing refused to speak, it only leered as if in a daze at the stunned patrons at the bar.

The two sisters hid behind the understandably confused-looking living young man. He squinted through the thin realm membrane most likely baffled by the hazy view of these unusual afterlife events. Mary looked for the soldier; he was gone. He must have fled the carriage. This unusual situation concerned Mary but intrigued her more. Why was this oddly behaved Soul Reaper here? What did it want? She took a final sip, placed her thumb and forefinger on her talisman pendant, and stood, determined to find out what this creature needed.

5

I f the well-weathered bartender was at all alarmed, he hid it well, calmly drying a glass and cheekily enquiring, "What do you drink, my friend?"

The creature stopped and made an unearthly sound, like a growl, and slowly plodded toward them. Its massive skeletal form beneath dark robes knocked over incidental cocktail tables and chairs as it made a beeline to the bar.

From across the room, the bartender squinted, looked him up and down, and side to side. He called out, "I haven't seen you on this route today. Would you mind showing me your ticket?"

The creature ignored him.

Challenging the beast's imposition, Luis insisted, "You are no Soul Reaper, are you?"

It didn't respond.

"If you have no ticket, you must leave my lounge car, sorry."

Mary said, "Wait. Let me talk to him." She confidently strolled across the car, holding up an open palm as a show of goodwill and asked, "What do you need? Are you in trouble?"

This was Mary's bread and butter. She could charm the most gruesome of troubled spirits and ghouls.

Behind Mary, she heard Luis set down the glass and make a shifting sound. She looked back and saw he had hopped over the bar. He stood with a pristine, folded bar towel draped over his left shoulder, a firm grip on his muddler, and well prepared to assist if diplomacy turned to violence.

The creature responded by reaching out to Mary, unfurling thick skeletal fingers. Its jaw dislocated and dropped wide open as it let out a low, menacing groan like a howling wolf. The wall of noise grew louder, transforming into a most horrible multitonal shriek, as if all the keys of an enormous pipe organ were pressed simultaneously. Mary winced at the horrible sound, but amongst the noise she heard a slow, sinister voice. "Mary, I came here for you!"

This set Mary back; a chill ran through her.

The black smoke that accompanied the monster spread out to the sides of the car, avoiding Mary, and gathered menacingly near the patrons like henchmen prepared to hold the group hostage. Alarmed, the sisters sat up, then climbed on the bar to avoid it. Mary wanted to know more.

"If you are here for me, leave them alone. I will follow you off the train at the next stop and we can talk."

Her words garnered no response from the creature, and it continued to advance toward her. She sensed a barely conscious, tortured soul and alarmingly genuine wicked intension that she hadn't felt since leaving the living realm. A familiar morbid sensation like cold spiders climbing up and down her spine sprung up, and she stumbled as she stepped backward.

"Who are you?" she asked, horrified, her voice now trembling.

"I am responsible for the safety of my lounge, Mary. Let me handle this," Luis said.

She didn't want to quarrel with him, but she was uncertain if the bartender could handle the monster, and despite her sense of dread, she had to know more about this thing.

As the creature neared Mary, the thick creeping mist it emitted had completely blanketed the floor of the cabin to knee height, and its tendrils began reaching over the top of the bar threatening the sisters. Luis had to act. He moved past Mary, holding his glowing, enchanted bar towel up to his face, and in his other hand, his charmed muddler. Just as the beast was about to speak again, Luis swung the muddler at the monster, striking its face and releasing an energy blast. The beast fell back and pulled with it the thickest core of the mist, which gathered up toward the monster. It was like a giant black octopus in retreat.

The bartender advanced again, but the beast extended his long arm and clutched Luis's wrist before he could swipe again. It turned its head to him and ejected a thick black jet from its jaws, enveloping the bartender's head in a toxic swirl of fume and soot. He swung his head side to side, but the plume seemed to have latched on.

Mary stepped forward to intervene, but before she could

act, the creature threw Luis to the side, hurtling toward the legs of an overturned cocktail table. The bartender, blinded by the acrid smoke, took one last vain swipe, but only disturbed air. He crashed hard and tangled into the table legs, dropping both his muddler and towel. With an undefended target, the deranged Soul Reaper released another torrent of smoke that engulfed Luis's head and he collapsed to the floor, writhing, smothered by the cloudy mass.

Mary gripped her pendant and, with all her will, threw energy of intention blasting out from her other hand, outstretched to blindside the beast. Her powerful blue bolt struck the center of the Soul Reaper's chest, and it blasted straight through the wall of the train car, without damaging it. As the Reaper went, it pulled the thickest core of its toxic fumes out with it. Mary ran to the window to see flickers of light, smoke, and twisted-off foliage erupt as the creature tumbled through the dark forest.

Mary turned her attention to the injured bartender lying in great distress. He was already attended to by Barbara, who was sitting on the floor holding his head in her lap. All attempts to comfort him were in vain. He violently choked and gagged, then took a tiny breath, but then choked again. His wide eyes stared at Mary as his head convulsed. Mary used the power of her pendent to hover off the ground and soar through the carriages to reach her cabin for her bag. When she returned, the train began to slow for its approach to Frankfurt.

Bits of dark mist that remained did not have the animated living motion they had before, but still reeked, causing the spirits inside to cough and gag. The ticket agent rushed into the cabin and approached the side door. With a hand firmly on the lever of a boarding door leading outside, the agent inserted and turned a thick key. Doors on both sides of the train pushed out and slid open to the noise of the rails and wind outside. The toxic smoke was quickly sucked out of the car and the doors shut again.

"We have to do something for him!" said Barbara.

Luis was still choking, turning shades of blue. Mary knelt beside him and opened her bag, rifling through the compartment of glass vials for some elixir to ease his pain. The ticket agent stood over her, looking frustrated.

"What is this? Why is he not getting better?" the agent asked.

"I'm afraid he has Death Cough," Mary said.

"Death Cough?"

"Yes, Soul Reapers carry souls between the living and the afterlife realms," Mary said as she nervously opened three vials from her bag and poured them into an empty bar glass. "The exposure to the Reaper's trans-dimensional mist has left him trapped between realms. He suffocates but cannot die." Mary paused as the horror hit her. "He is caught in an eternal coughing loop."

"Aren't you a guardian? You should have been able to prevent this!" the agent said sternly. The agent shouted something urgently in German into a communication device as the train entered the station. Mary desperately tended to Luis, administering various combinations of potions hoping for something to ease his suffering. Nothing could be done to stop the choking, and no amount of painkiller can make perpetual suffocating comfortable. Desperate to bring him some comfort, she tried to sedate him. He writhed less violently, but his eyes still darted about the room, desperately pleading for relief. He looked into her eyes, and Mary wanted to look away, but she didn't. Instead, she could only tearfully apologize.

Physical suffering in the afterlife was rare, and this was a harrowing scene.

Laura pulled at Barbara's arm. "Let's go back to our seats. This is too awful to watch."

Barbara stood, and the two slowly backed away.

"That thing was pure evil," Barbara said.

"What the hell was wrong with that Soul Reaper?" Laura screamed with outrage.

As the sobbing sisters attempted to depart, a team of local responders stopped their exit and entered the disheveled lounge car. Some took over tending to the bartender, and a group of investigators announced that they all needed to stay for questioning. Mary knew she could do nothing for Luis. She closed her bag and was escorted to a table to be questioned.

Barbara and Laura sat down at a cocktail table and gave statements to another investigator, sometimes looking at Mary as they spoke in hushed tones. Mary sheepishly revealed that she was the guardian of the Tragically Dead in Amsterdam, on her way to Prague.

Her compassionate but fruitless attempts to communicate with the beast, rather than do more to protect the crew and passengers, felt unforgivable. Mary told them what happened accurately, only leaving out that she thought she heard the beast say it was there for her.

Passengers in other cars were alarmed but began complaining about being held up and those seeking to investigate the trouble were blocked from entering the lounge car. The shame of the situation gutted Mary. After she explained what happened, she returned to her cabin in shock.

The train emerged from the dense forest, and a gray sky reflected off the wet tracks. News of the encounter with the beast had made its way throughout the afterlife train, with exaggerations and slight twists on what happened.

The train turned southeast toward the center of the Bohemian afterlife.

Just as her tolerance for sitting aboard the train had nearly run out, it pulled into Prague's central station. Mary stepped off the train, then turned down the concrete platform and rolled her bag toward the station's vast and extravagant domed hall. Thick with the living realm's shadow-shapes of neurotic commuters eagerly scurrying away from work for the evening, Mary dashed through the humid space.

She exited the congested station to the open outdoors where the air was fresh but chilly. Setting out, she wanted to forget what happened on the train. It had been years since she last visited Prague. She hoped now to remember the most efficient route through the unavoidably surreptitious interchange of narrow stone streets to reach the Church of Our Lady before *Týn* in Old Town Square.

6

Aal raced through Amsterdam's canals savoring the sensation of the murky, chilly currents coursing over his pale skin. After sprinting a few extra laps, the eel was reasonably certain that Darkhorse would have returned to the house, and he wanted to follow up after the eventful morning. His body glowed and changed width as he ascended from the canal through the dark pipes and entered the interior of the canal house via the drain of the kitchen sink. Soapy warm water passed by him, and he emerged with a cap of foam atop his head.

"Hey, Aal," said a mouse, chuckling.

"Hello, my friend. Helping wash teacups?"

"Doing my best!"

With a flick of his fin, Aal mysteriously refilled the sink with warm soapy water in an instant. "Is Darkhorse in his room?"

"No, he's staring at the old photos again."

"Ah, thank you." Aal slithered off the counter crowded with sudsy mice and turned down the hall.

Around the corner from the large kitchen, he found Darkhorse gazing at the framed memories covering the expanse of the wall almost from floor to ceiling. They were a hodgepodge of framed photos, drawings, paintings, and etchings commemorating the centuries of the Tragically Dead who had passed through or were currently in recovery. Many classes of the animal kingdom were on display – kind spirits from centuries of history. Some images depicted an individual's time among the living, others depicted their time here in the Amsterdam afterlife.

"Isn't it something?" Aal said. "The sheer number of glorious memories. It is always a pleasure to gaze upon this wall."

"Yes, it is," Darkhorse said.

Aal was concerned that Darkhorse seemed to be transfixed on one photo.

"This was taken the day I joined Amsterdam's noble fire brigade."

Darkhorse once again revisited the quaint grainy image familiar to Aal: Darkhorse, alive and strong in 1919; a proud, handsome young horse, strapped to state-of-the-art equipment; a steam-powered fire pump standing on wagon wheels; and seated atop, a group of mustachioed, uniformed men. Their eyes gazed out from a century ago, under sepia-toned shadows cast by their helmets.

Darkhorse said, "I was a firefighter for less than a month before it happened. I thought I was a hero. I thought I would be remembered for saving people. The most notable aspect of my life, the thing I am most remembered for, is how I died. What was it all for?"

Aal understood well the details of that first call. Those were the last moments of Darkhorse's life. The narrow streets weren't made to be navigated by a speeding horse wagon. Circumstances were such that as they barreled west over a small bridge to answer a call, they failed to slow enough to make the turn and crashed mightily into a crowded café.

"They all died because of me," Darkhorse said flatly.

The eel paused for a moment.

"Darkhorse, you should be proud of your life. You acted with a brave selflessness in the service the people of Amsterdam, dying nobly as a fire horse in the line of duty. We all admire the life you lived. You should too."

Gazing down at his hooves, Darkhorse stood in silence.

The eel continued softly, "You may not realize it, but just like Mary and me, you are a key figure of the Tragically Dead in Recovery. You've become more essential here every day, to the point where we can't imagine not having you here."

As the mid-morning light entered the hallway, Darkhorse looked back up and peered at his skeletal reflection in the glass.

"I'm grateful for you and Mary. You have been supporting me for a long time, and I realize that I need to have more gratitude for what I have here," Darkhorse said. "I try to avoid dwelling on negativity by focusing on what I have, by concentrating on the good things that are present. It had been going well until recently. I forgot that today and fell pretty hard into a spiral of despair." The two stood in silence for a moment. "Aal, you're a good friend. Thank you for rescuing me. I value your encouragement and friendship."

To give comfort, the eel's body embraced the solemn horse spirit, and then returned to rest his chin on Darkhorse's shoulder.

"You are making better progress than you realize," Aal reassured him.

They stood there for a few moments before recalling their knowledge of the subjects on the wall. Darkhorse asked about some pictures of Aal that he said he'd just noticed for the first time. He said he was familiar with the ubiquitous print depicting the 1886 Eel Riots. The days of rioting made international news, and a French newspaper had commissioned this etching, depicting the day Aal died, strung up over *Lindengracht* in an "eel pulling" competition. He pointed to the one with Aal posing with the Queen of the Netherlands, but said he'd never noticed the one of Aal in a tweed jacket, lecturing to dead scholars at a university, or in India meditating next to the yogi, Paramahansa Yogananda. Aal conceded that those were just added in the last few decades, so they were rather new.

When there was just the right moment in the conversation, Aal said, "Mary wants us to let the house know that she has headed to Prague for a rescue and we should assemble the housemates to prepare for the new arrival today or tomorrow."

As the sky brightened, various dead awakened and Darkhorse asked others to help gather everyone from each floor and assemble in the large main room. A raucous few minutes of relaying the call to assemble echoed throughout the five stories. Finally, everyone crammed into the great room.

When Aal informed them of the new arrival, they cheered and chattered among themselves for a few seconds. The birds said they were delighted to have another feathered member.

Darkhorse clopped his hooves together loudly to get them to quiet down so they could create an action plan.

In celebration of the new arrival, the tea committee would prepare a special meal. Fawn, the doe, volunteered to gather art supplies to create a welcome banner. As usual she drafted Gerald, her best friend, to take her on his bike. The laid-back rhino smiled and agreed genially as if he had a choice. Everyone was aware that the spirited doe had grown possessively fond of the gentle rhinoceros in the months since she'd arrived. They were an odd couple, but as Aal put it, Gerald had "the patience of a saint" and appeared glad to be a supportive and kind role model to the volatile little doe.

As frequently happens with house meetings, the discussion became mired in some logistical arguments, dominated mainly by where the new member might most likely prefer to sleep. With the important tasks assigned and realizing that the meeting was derailed, Darkhorse excused himself, returning to the sanctuary of his bedroom. Aal refocused them on more important points, and the gathering ended without a firm conclusion on that subject. Eventually, the dead left the large room and redistributed themselves throughout the house, chattering excitedly. Gerald and Fawn invited Aal to join them, and he agreed, but on the condition that Darkhorse be invited.

"Oh great, we have to bring along Pity-Pony?" the callous little doe complained.

"Yes, today is his Deathday. Do this for me," Gerald said calmly.

"Fine," she reluctantly agreed.

"Great, we'll meet you two downstairs," Aal said.

Gerald and Fawn descended the stairs to the front door, and Aal went down the hall to Darkhorse's bedroom. After much reassurance and encouragement (and a promise of ice cream), Aal finally coaxed Darkhorse out.

They descended the stairs onto the stoop to see Fawn and Gerald standing beside the bike. The eel hovered past Darkhorse and glided gently into the bike's basket.

Darkhorse paused at the open front door. "I forgot to...I have something upstairs I need to get."

"That is fine, we will wait for you," assured the eel.

Darkhorse disappeared back up the stairs.

"Come on, why is he like this?" Fawn implored.

"Try to show some empathy," the rhino whispered to her. "We are in no rush."

"At least you are driving and not Mary. She must be the slowest bicyclist in Amsterdam."

Aal and Gerald smiled to one another. They knew the horse's spirit well. Aal heard the light in Darkhorse's room flick off and on again several times, then the lock.

He trotted down the stairs and emerged muttering, "I am safe, I am in control." He repeated the self-talk mantra as he methodically stepped down the stoop.

The doe was as patient as she could be, holding back the cruel onslaught of barbs and jabs she would have been tempted to deliver if not in the company of the rhino and eel she so respected.

Straddling his bike, the rhinoceros invited Darkhorse to stand on pegs attached to the rear frame and place his hooves on the outside of Gerald's shoulders for balance. Darkhorse froze for a moment before Aal reassured him that he would use his mystic powers to ensure their safety. The eel smiled up assuring, seated in the basket in front of the handlebars and gesturing with his fin for Darkhorse to take his assigned place on the bike behind the enormous rhino. Finally, the rhino lifted the young spotted doe and draped her around his neck in the usual way, with her hind legs on his left shoulder, her front legs on his right. She rested her chin on the crown of his head as the four spirited away along the canal.

Gerald's powerful legs churned, and the group gathered speed until they were racing along the canal. He slowed to a cruise as they turned off and entered a crowded space but couldn't avoid intersecting with some living forms who jumped in alarm at what was likely the great sensation of chills from four souls and a bike from the afterlife swiftly passing through them.

"That'll wake them up!" Fawn shouted. Everyone but Darkhorse chuckled. "Hey, turn onto Rokin so we can really move!" she commanded.

Rokin was a wide street with an ample bike lane, and Gerald was happy to oblige. The sensation of speeding along again was delightful. Despite his usual aversion to velocity, even Darkhorse seemed to be enjoying it.

Approaching the art studio, Gerald popped the bike up onto the edge of the pavement, and they soared above the ground until skidding into a spot next to the entrance.

"Yeah!" Fawn exclaimed.

"Nice landing," Darkhorse quipped dryly, and quickly stepped off the bike and back onto terra firma.

He accidentally bumped into the gallery's sandwich board. None but Aal noticed it was about to fall over, and the eel stopped it with his mind, discreetly setting it back to a stable position.

Gerald hopped off the bike and leaned down so the doe could dismount off his shoulders. They all entered the art studio gallery through an open garage door and spread out for a moment to check out the latest installment of paintings by a visiting artist. The subjects of the oil paintings were mainly architectural. The style was painterly, with pleasingly rough brush strokes, vividly depicting the dead artist's travels to Mexico, Spain, and Italy.

A lovely blonde woman with a kind smile stepped into the space and addressed Fawn as if this was her first time in the gallery. "Well hello there. Welcome. Let me know if you have any questions."

Fawn gave the woman a look as if the doe had smelled something rotten.

The woman continued anyway. "Where are you visiting Amsterdam from?"

Fawn seemed to be doing her best to not be too rude in front of Gerald and Aal.

"Thanks, but we're here to see our good friend *Zono*." She said the name of the permanent main artist at the studio, indicating through a condescending vocal tone, that she was quite familiar with the place. Zono was an immensely talented boar who Fawn had befriended last year. Introduced by Aal at an exhibit opening, the two became fast friends.

The feisty little doe turned her nose up and brushed past the smiling woman, who looked puzzled by Fawn's reaction. The woman looked to Gerald, who grinned in sympathy and shrugged his shoulders. "We live here. On *Herengracht*," he said.

Aal saw all this out of the corner of his eye but was taken by the brushwork texture of the paintings through his spirit-glass monocle. He remarked, "This artist started this painting when he was alive and finished it when he was dead."

"Yes, isn't that interesting," the woman said.

"These are marvelous! I have not seen this artist before. I think I am his newest fan!" Aal adored everything about the unique paintings. They were the perfect gifts for the well-known hosts he would be staying with on his upcoming Grand Tour, so he put several on reserve.

A few minutes later, Fawn emerged from the back of the studio. She held a bag filled with art supplies; its handles pinched between her teeth. Without acknowledging the woman, the doe trotted straight out the door. Gerald and Aal thanked the woman, gathered Darkhorse, who was admiring a painting of a night scene, and headed out.

Fawn stood waiting and gave the bag to Gerald, who placed the art supplies in the front basket of the bicycle.

"Is there still enough room for you in there, Aal?" Gerald asked.

"Yes, not a problem," said Aal, and he shrunk his body to around eighty percent of his regular size to sit comfortably inside the basket with the supplies.

Darkhorse said, "Let's get some ice cream."

"Heck yes," Fawn agreed, "I'm with him!" She looked up and noted how tall Darkhorse was standing on the bicycle pegs. "How's the view up there, Darkhorse?"

"Not bad, why?"

"Could I ride on your shoulders? I always wanted to be tall."

"Sure, um, I suppose," he replied.

Gerald helped as she climbed up onto Darkhorse's shoulders. She couldn't see over his head if she perched on him the way she did on the rhino's thick neck, so she repositioned herself with her rear hooves standing on the dead equine's shoulders and with her front ones jammed in the ear holes atop his head, allowing her own head to rest on top.

"This is cool. *Oké*, Gerald, we're set," Fawn said.

"What?" asked Darkhorse, and they took off, stopping for some ice cream before returning home.

7

M ary saw a row of Prague's ornamental streetlights all illuminate at once. Their glow reflected off the wet ground and the multitude of shapes from the city's diverse architecture. There was a lull between showers when she arrived, but cold winds blew across the Vltava river, howling as they channeled through the damp, narrow streets. The chill bit at Mary but couldn't quite get to her. She was well insulated against the cold nip, bundled in her thick black woolen cape and cowl. Just the tip of her nose barely exposed to the damp wind. Thunder rolled across the city, announcing that another onslaught of icy rain could resume at any time.

Guided initially by intuition, Mary soon realized she was on the right course when she recognized a key landmark. Jerusalémská lane hosted the grand Jubilee Synagogue adorned with a unique Moorish revival style. Seeing it was always a treat, even if she didn't have time to go inside. She stopped in front of it and admired its splendor through the pale fog of her breath, then continued.

Finally, she stepped onto *Celetná*, a twisted black-and-white stone street lined with bookstores, restaurants, and boutiques, leading directly to the *Týn* cathedral. She passed an enchanting toy store, a frequent haunt for Aal, who appreciated both the whimsy of its contents as well as the arc of Art Nouveau lettering advertising it.

At the end of the narrow promenade, *Týn*'s impressive twin cathedral towers came into view. Mary's heart leaped at seeing *Týn* again. Equally symmetric series of narrow, triangular steeples crowned the two tall Gothic towers, adorned with eight smaller, similarly sharp versions of the two main towers. It created a visual chorus of arrows, stretching up to the sky. They appeared to Mary as if even more narrow this time, more like giant iron pikes yearning to touch the foreboding clouds above.

She progressed briskly as light showers began, and soon she could see the near end of the vaulted roof of the cathedral's ambulatory central aisle. An attachment of tall enforcements surrounded it, and between them a series of tall narrow windows with pointed tops. Once she reached the massive cathedral, she turned right. After rounding the circumference to reach its north entrance gate, she admired the finely carved marble relief above the thick wooden door.

A heavy thud came from behind the door, followed by the slow creaking of the hinges as it receded into the dim hollows of the cathedral's vast interior. The cloaked figure of Mary's associate, Jerome, emerged from the dark and glided down the stone steps. He clasped a black rose in his burnt skeleton hands. The shoulders of his heavy dark robes took on raindrops, and he emerged as if melting through the cold metal bars, meeting no resistance.

Mary smiled, accepted the large black rose and, in a continental fashion, casually pecked each of Jerome's scarred cheeks. They passed through the iron of the locked gate and headed up the steps to enter the vast, dimly lit cathedral.

Jerome raised his scorched skeletal hands, each manifesting a bright flame to illuminate their passage. Mary and Jerome went down the long aisle to another doorway leading to the base of the main towers, then ascended the great series of narrow spiral staircases toward the afterlife section. Rain tapped at the stone and stained glass, creating a soft noise in the background of their steady footsteps.

Mary used her night vision discretely to supplement what Jerome's torch-emitting hands couldn't entirely illuminate. As she ascended several more floors, she admired how every little cranny and corner had been crafted into study nooks of various magnitudes, to suit the variety of sizes and species of scholars. The subjects of study varied. Some desks contained small artifacts under suspended spyglass for examination. Others held manuscripts and texts.

As they progressed, Mary passed the first group, a pair of squirrel scholars scribbling at a station. The workspace they occupied was ample, designed for a much larger species, but their task required the extra space. Drafting a schematic, they carefully dissected an intricate gold-metallic device full of tiny gears, pins and armature. It appeared to be perhaps a clock or compass; Mary couldn't be sure. They'd laid the device's multitude of tiny intricate machine elements out on a grid, each part meticulously labeled.

As she continued, various other species dutifully hunched over their studies, reading and taking notes on various historical manuscripts, pamphlets or scrolls.

Jerome locked his hands behind him. "We have a tragically dead raven who came into afterlife consciousness just a few hours ago. The sweet soul is recovering as best he can in my study. They killed him north of Holland in Friesland at some world record domino-stacking competition. My young scholars who witnessed his death are fresh to the afterlife, so they were uncertain of what to do with him. With only tickets to return to Prague, I'm afraid they passed right through Amsterdam on their way home. If they'd had more experience, they would have stopped to see you and saved you the trip."

"No need to apologize. My journey was pleasant albeit unexpectedly exciting, and it is always a delight to visit Prague."

The two continued up another long set of passages to ascend the thinner tower.

"I assume Aal will soon depart for another one of his *Grand Tours*?" Jerome asked.

During his first century in recovery, the eel once stayed for an extended period in the tower, studying with Jerome. He had an unquenchable thirst for knowledge, reading everything he could get his tiny fins on before moving on to the London Library to further expand the depth of his studies.

Mary smiled at the thought of her dear friend. "He will depart in a few days. I will miss him. He has been a steadfast mentor and deserves a few months off on his adventures."

"Aal is one of a kind. That he remains in the afterlife realm to so selflessly serve amazes me; he could have advanced long ago. His devotion to the betterment of this realm is a testament to his character."

"I find him to be a great mentor and an essential asset. I don't know what I'd do without his generous guidance and wisdom. He seems to always pop up when I need him most," Mary said.

The two turned and headed down a suspended hallway to yet a smaller tower that finally led to a vast afterlife reading space. Jerome unlatched a wooden door, and there before Mary, the core group of scholars were engaged in various intellectual pursuits, surrounded by stacks of suspended books and scrolls. The combined light of a conjured central fire pit and a galaxy of hovering study lamps illuminated the vast arrangement of studious animal spirits, each busy directly or in support of another's scholarly pursuit. Mountains of notes and open manuscripts in multiple languages were piled up on the desks.

Mary followed Jerome around the edge of the room toward his office. The focus and attention of the diverse menagerie always impressed her. Only one scholar, a rabbit wearing bifocals, paused briefly to look up at Mary. He twitched his nose and promptly buried it back in the book he was studying.

In the afterlife, each soul was free to pursue what most inspired them. They yearned, more than anything, to continue their pursuit of knowledge, and Jerome's haven enabled them to do just that.

Scholarly mice scurried back and forth, noses down, speed-reading the text of the large books. They moved like tiny turbocharged plows working a field. Among them, a pair of these mice diligently teamed up to relay the page's contents to an impaired badger named Jan. As one mouse assistant scurried down Jan's furry left arm to read the page, the other ran up his right to stand on his shoulder and relay the text from the previous page directly into his ear as the other read the next.

This rodential reading service enabled a continuous stream of information for the knowledge-hungry badger to absorb. The sweet and supportive nature of the dead always delighted Mary.

Jerome led Mary into his study at the darker end of the circular stone room. Cluttered with books and artifacts spread about on several desks, the other furniture in his office included two massive antique globes (one celestial and one terrestrial) and a sleeping bunk. He directed Mary's attention to a far corner where an arched window was protected by massive wooden slats. Outside the darkness of evening had descended and it was raining hard.

Just below the window on a small table rested the young raven draped in a soft blanket. He gently wept, both wings crossed, their feathers intertwined covering his head. The "cool rain" code meant that the subject was an airborne creature who had entered the afterlife with a disfigured spirit-form, and "fog" signified that the death had been intentional and unjust.

Mary approached carefully. "Hello, I am Mary van Amsterdam. I am here to help you."

His wings nudged just enough that one of the bird's shiny black eyes could peer up at her.

"What name do you prefer to go by?" she asked.

"I chose Tycho as an afterlife name." The raven's voice quivered.

"Tycho, are you in physical pain?"

"Bill is sore, and stinks."

Confused, Mary looked to Jerome, who was standing back near the door of the study. "He intends to say his bill stings."

"Ah, well to start, I can relieve your physical pain quickly. This is an astonishingly effective, fast-acting elixir."

As Mary removed a small vial from her bag and unscrewed the lid, remembering how she'd failed to ease Luis's suffering, a shock of guilt ran through her, but she pressed on for the sake of the whimpering raven. She bent over, holding a dropper of elixir toward him, but the shy bird suddenly retreated, turning away and desperately concealing his face behind his wings.

"Tycho, darling, this pain is not worth enduring. This elixir is harmless and will ease your suffering."

Mary's assurances worked, and the traumatized raven re-emerged slowly. Through parted feathers, she saw one of the bird's eyes peeking at her, but it obscured its beak. Then she calmly coaxed him to show her his second eye. Mary's eyes glowed blue as she peered deeply into the raven's eyes. Hypnotized, he stared up at her, and she began to read his soul.

She took a journey into the history of the spirit's consciousness, chronologically, but in reverse. From his perspective she felt his pain, his regrets, she heard a gunshot. Before that, amazement and playful freedom, the joy of soaring among thermals and diving beside cliffs. These specific joys sustained the bird's spirit. Before that, his dive out of the nest and the bright emergence from within the cracking shell of his mother's egg. Then, darkness, and soon, the end of his life before he was a raven – as a sick old human dying in a cold lonely place, locked away and surviving on scraps but sharing what little he had with others. Before that some sort of sentence predicated on an unjust trial, conducted by a corrupt court, and before that a capture, then the chase, a long period where he felt abandoned and rejected, and on and on, through more lives as other species.

Mary also experienced his lives branch out and then splice together, a rich tapestry of full and partial lives that all combined to form what was Tycho. She confirmed that indeed he had experienced an inordinate series of consecutively unjust existences to qualify him to join the Tragically Dead in Recovery. Not only that, but in each life, he suffered such incredible series of injustices, and yet in each one, he consistently shared all he had and resisted letting his suffering make him selfish. Mary made the final call; he was due for an enhanced afterlife experience as the case code had implied. But first, she endeavored to get him through the night.

8

It was not just the physical pain of his injury that was causing the raven such distress, but there was shame from the trauma that Mary also needed to address. Physical pain makes any task less achievable. Mary plucked a large petal from the fragrant black rose Jerome had given her.

She held it out to Tycho. "I will pour a dose of this 'Painless Potion' into one of these and set it down and go back to the other end of the room. Take a sip from it whenever you are ready. Then, we can continue healing the rest of you when you are not in so much pain, and we can get you ready. There is an amazing time in store for you in the afterlife."

Placing several drops of the potion into the black flower petal, she placed it down in front of the cowering raven and walked back over to Jerome, who was standing at the other end of the room.

"Would it be a bother if I stayed here with him for the night?" she asked Jerome softly.

"Of course not. There is a large overstuffed chair and ottoman there you may rest in if need be," he said. "I will tend to my scholars tonight."

"Thank you, my friend," Mary said.

The little bird suddenly sang out boldly but with his speech again affected by his injury, "Biss Bary, I ab a'ready peeling buch bedder bow."

Jerome and Mary exchanged smiles, and he exited the room so that the two could begin recovery.

Mary returned and sat with the bird. "Tycho, I am here in the afterlife to guide you through the rest of your recovery personally. We can communicate with thoughts and words, so you don't have to speak if you don't want to, I can hear your thoughts if you direct them to me."

"Okay," said the raven.

"To get started, all we have to do is communicate about what happened to you and how it made you feel. Would that be all right?"

"Sure, wow, you can hear me thinking?"

"Yes, what do you remember from your departure from the living realm?"

"Dey shot be." He said aloud, forgetting that Mary could hear his thought.

"Were you alone?"

"No, the guy who shot me was there," the raven thought as he concentrated at Mary.

"Right, well. Were there any other birds or animals around?"

The raven looked at Mary for a moment and focused his thoughts, communicating: "No, there were just a lot of humans. See, I was exploring this vast human interior, filled with the most amazing small standing stones!"

Mary saw a vision of the large series of colorful rooms. She recognized that dominoes were lined up on a massive scale.

"Wow, this was near you in Friesland?"

"Yes, I was flying around, near where I hatched, when I spotted a familiar building with an open window. Heat was wafting out, and when I flew through the warm air, it felt so nice. Finally, I just flew on through the window. Inside I found an incredible series of large colorful rooms with amazing sculptures and arrangements of items. The floors were filled with winding rows of smooth flat stones, lined up in some ritualistic manner, like soldiers marching shoulder to shoulder in some places. They glimmered and were amazing. I attempted to get a closer look. There were so many! I had to have one for myself, surely they wouldn't miss just one." The raven winced, and Mary felt through the ether echoes of his deep sense of shame.

"Shiny things are attractive to your species. You shouldn't feel bad, Tycho, just take your time. What happened next?"

"I flew down and plucked one. Someone swiped at me with a thick branch with a bundle of reeds at the end. When I dodged, I dropped the flat stone, and it hit another one, it fell and hit another one, and another, creating a loud sound like a massive waterfall. It went on for some time. This infuriated the people. They didn't want me there and chased me with nets and blankets. I can take a hint, you know. So, I flew back to the window, but it was locked. I searched for an exit desperately. Getting tired, I pleaded for mercy, but they kept throwing things at me. It was truly terrifying, Mary. I had no choice but to stay in the air until I could fly no more. Then some guy came in with a gun and shot me! So much more I wanted to do. I am only a juvenile, you know? Why didn't they just let me out?"

"I am so sorry, Tycho. You died young and without good reason." *I can relate, more than you know.* She swallowed hard, empathizing with the little bird by silently recalling personal regrets kept close to her heart, then continued, "We cannot change the past, but this is not the end. This trip to the afterlife has a lot more to offer you than you have previously experienced. This is just the beginning. As your assigned guardian, I can assure you that some amazing things are in store for you. The afterlife exists so you can be happy."

"How can I be happy like this?" Tycho asked in his mind.

"What do you mean?" asked Mary.

The bird parted his wings, revealing a grim wound where his absent beak should attach to his face. His tongue rested in the middle of a mass of coagulated blood and shattered tissue and the ragged shell of the upper and lower remains of his beak. It was a wonder he could speak at all.

"Mary... I am missing half my head," the bird communicated and sobbed.

She patiently talked with the traumatized dead bird for several hours, learning about his life and slowly sharing the unexpected delights the afterlife could offer him. It was getting very late. Tomorrow she would take him to the nearest repository – there was one at Prague castle – and get Tycho set up to enhance his experience in the afterlife. Then the two could return to Amsterdam. But for now, Mary kicked her shoes off and lounged comfortably in a large overstuffed chair.

Bonds form quickly when communicating silently, and after an emotional night of gentle discourse and assurances, Tycho nestled his tear-soaked head into Mary's comforting arms. High in the warm tower of the cathedral, the two fell into a deep, well-earned sleep as dead scholars scribbled and studied just outside the study, well into the stormy night.

Mary slept rather soundly though intermittently, considering the turmoil the day had thrust upon her. Her guilt about disappointing Darkhorse was eased when she remembered how wise and reliable Aal was. But that problem was soon replaced by the shame of failing to protect Luis from the estranged Soul Reaper. The clumsily destructive creature reminded her of her time in the living realm, the terror of war she endured for so long. The anxiety of hiding, but also the bonds it created.

She remembered Peter more vividly than she ever had since arriving in the afterlife. While she eventually dismissed his affection toward the end of their friendship, earlier on she couldn't imagine her life with any other boy. She remembered his eyes and his sweet smile. They'd lie down together and stare up at the chestnut tree, listening to the bell from the *Westerkerk* and imagining what their life together would be like when the war ended and they would be adults.

The pleasant memory was interrupted by the horror of Luis choking in perpetuity. What kind of guardian was she? Mary always felt she handled her duties better as a healer than a warrior, and she would have to settle the score by doing everything in her spare time to help find a treatment for that condition. She feared she would struggle to find the time, barely managing to juggle the duties of treating the Tragically Dead as it stood, let alone assigning herself the burden of discovering a cure for Death Cough.

AT DAWN, Prague's sky glowed a soft gray, visible through the narrow east window of the cathedral's tower chamber. Mary slowly awoke and peered down to see if Tycho was awake. Tilting his head, Tycho blinked before setting it back down in the warm crook of Mary's arm.

Yawning and stretching apart the stubby cracked-off remnants of his shattered bill, Tycho began his second day in the afterlife. The night before, Mary comforted him with reassurances that today they would remedy his damaged bill.

When he awoke, Mary offered Tycho the safety of withdrawing to the private comfort and seclusion of her black handbag. Making himself at home, Tycho seemed comfortable reclining in a pair of black-and-white silk scarves. With the injured bird in tow, she carefully made her way past the desks of snoring dead scholars. Jerome approached, surrounded by a small contingent of intrigued early risers.

"Good morning, Mary. Are you heading to the station?" Jerome handed Mary one of the two hot cups he was holding.

"Good morning, Jerome. Yes, but first we are taking a special trip up the hill to the castle. The Duke will have just the right artifact for Tycho," Mary replied.

"That's wonderful. Tycho is a worthy recipient of his craft," Jerome replied, and they each took a sip of their steaming hot tea.

One scholar's assistant, a designated page-turner in the form of an adolescent orange-and-white cat, briefly stretched her front paws out in front of her then effortlessly hopped from a table and with soft steps, approached Mary. The kitten's delicate thin tail stood high in the air as she looked up and addressed Mary.

"Good morning," the kitten said.

"Hello there," Mary replied. "I haven't met you before."

"You are Mary van Amsterdam, aren't you?"

"Yes, I am. What are you called, little kitten?"

"I'm Agatha. I just arrived in the afterlife last October, but my friends and I are great admirers of you and your work with the Tragically Dead in Recovery."

"Is that so? Well, thank you, Agatha!"

"You helped our friend Basil, and he told us all about you before his graduation."

"Oh, Basil is a sweet soul. Thank you so much, Agatha. That is one of the kindest things anyone has ever said to me. Any friend of Basil's is always welcome for a visit to us in

Amsterdam. The house has fond memories of him. Visit any time."

Kneeling, Mary shook the sweet kitten's paw and excused herself. The kitten rejoined the charming, informal farewell assembly, who then wished Mary and Tycho a safe journey. With Tycho riding in her bag, Mary followed Jerome down the long, hollow buttress high atop the cathedral tower.

At the landing near the stairwell, Jerome handed Mary two hot, fresh rye rolls wrapped in a clean, white cloth napkin. His glowing-red skeletal hands had kept them warm, and she held the bundle up to her nose to savor the rich scent of the warm fermented grain.

Peering through the ports of Mary's large handbag, Tycho took in a deep breath. "Those smell good!" the bird thought.

The aroma of the rolls must have made it inside the bag. Jerome gently leaned down and moved his hand toward the side of the handbag, blessing the traumatized bird with wishes of safe travels, swift recovery, and well-being. Jerome was a kind guardian who always expressed great love, compassion, and genuine encouragement to Mary.

"Thank you, Jerome," Mary said.

"Safe travels, my friends. Oh, and tell Aal hello for me," replied Jerome.

"I will," she said. Just as when she arrived, Mary casually pecked Jerome on his cheeks and bid him farewell.

Leaving the warm upper floors behind, Mary descended the stone steps alone. Each level seemed colder than the last. Approaching the wooden exterior door, the frigid morning air crept under and bit at Mary's ankles. She opened the heavy entry door to find Old Town Prague blanketed in a thick fog.

Mary placed the warm rye bread in her bag with Tycho, keeping him warm and fed on their journey. When she suggested that he could get started on his first well-earned breakfast in the afterlife, he cooed in celebration.

Since his traumatic transition into the afterlife, he had likely worked up quite an appetite. He enthusiastically spread apart the folds of the warm napkin and pecked at the thick crust of one of the hot rustic rolls. He cursed aloud at his damaged beak and the hard bread crust. The bird fluttered and then stopped to sob.

Mary kindly propped her bag on a stone ledge, reached in and tore open the roll, revealing the steamy soft interior. Tycho thanked her, and his tears helped soak the bread so he could more easily chew it. Mary assured him they would get his condition remedied shortly and proceeded down the windy narrow streets, through the dense vapor.

As Tycho nibbled on soft morsels of rye, if he chose to, he could see well out of the vents of Mary's large handbag, specially designed for transporting injured creatures of his size. Approaching the river, the mist near the Charles Bridge was thinner. A complex series of centuries-old structures sat atop the knoll under a veil of morning haze.

As Mary crossed, the bridge felt empty, silent, and increasingly foreboding. On either side, statues towered over them— almost like they were leering down at them. Tycho quit munching when Mary stopped and took hold of her pendant, not sure what she was sensing exactly.

Something splashed out of the water and an unexpected serpentine form jumped at them through the fog.

9

I t was Aal. He appeared cheerily through the mist, and his full body slapped heartily before Mary against the stone before bouncing and positioning himself upright with his signature two-toothed grin.

"Hello, Mary!" he said with glee.

"Aal!" Mary replied, delighted, and relieved. "I am still always so surprised when you pop up! Do you have a portal near here?"

"Yes, during the Cold War, I'd placed a portal on the side of the bridge."

Mary tilted her handbag toward Aal, spreading it open with her hand so the two could see one another. "Aal, this is Tycho. Tycho, this is my mentor, Aal."

"How do you do, my friend?" Aal said warmly.

"Dice to beat you," Tycho replied in a shrill feeble voice, then groaned and retreated deeper inside the bag, and Mary closed it again.

"Nice to meet you as well!" the eel replied sincerely.

"Tycho passed into the afterlife while in Friesland, and Jerome's young scholars brought his soul way down here by train, unconscious."

"Alas, it gives us the opportunity to return to the wonderful sights of Prague," said Aal.

Mary explained that they were headed to the castle, and Aal celebrated. "Lucky bird! The Duke will set you right up, Tycho. You are in the best of hands, my friend."

"Would it be all right with you, Tycho, if Aal joined us?" Mary asked.

Seemingly taken aback that she was asking his permission, the raven stammered out, "Dat's fide."

They continued, and the eel floated just above the stones, which seemed to garner the attention of Tycho. Mary could feel him leaning to the side, peering out of the bag. Whenever Aal glanced over to the bag, the injured raven shifted back.

As they passed under the end of the bridge tower, the streets and pavement grew more crowded with morning tourists and commuters. Prague Castle was not a single structure but a complex of illustrious, haunted buildings high atop the hill. It included squares, palaces, halls, gardens, chapels and a lovely cathedral containing what the living considered the royal crown jewels.

Mary climbed the multiple sequences of well-worn stone steps lined with shops and cafés. Mary felt the bird press his face up to the vents in the bag, most likely to get a better look at the magical eel who, not suited for navigating stairs easily, used his abilities to levitate high above the steps at Mary's eye level. Mary too, soon tired of the stairs, opted to hover up through the morning mist.

"How high can you guys fwy?" Tycho asked in his soft nasally tone.

"Only a few feet above the ground," Mary replied. "It is useful when climbing many stairs."

"... and reduces the risk of tripping," added Aal with a knowing grin, which Mary returned.

At the crest of the hill, it leveled off. Mary and Aal made their way through the complex via several passages and vast squares, one containing a tall, embellished, stone and concrete plague monument tinted with a dark patina. An enchanted gate awaited them, and Mary tapped her necklace pendant against it in a certain spot. Aal then commented that the weather looked like it would clear up.

"Perhaps," Mary said, glancing up.

A boisterous, well-dressed man approached flanked by two tall, illuminated beings. He was well mannered with a pointy gray beard and a kind smile and displayed the formal mannerisms of dead royalty.

"Aal, Mary, how wonderful to see you!" the man said, greeting them enthusiastically.

They exchanged a short series of pleasantries, and he quickly invited them in. Mary referred to him as Duke, and Aal called him Val.

They followed through a series of long hallways and passed rows of guards – shorter versions of the ones who flanked the duke.

"Wow, I'b nebber been in a pace so shiny," Tycho said.

The Duke led the way to a large ornate ballroom with walls

and ceiling adorned. Mary set the handbag Tycho was resting in onto a baroque table featuring cabriole legs.

The Duke bowed and leaned his face next to the bag. "Hello, my friend. What is your name?"

"I ab Tycho." The bird's voice was nasally and muffled because of his injuries.

"Hello, Tycho. I am Duke Václav. You may call me Duke or Val, or whatever you'd prefer."

Tycho remained silent.

"I'd like to examine your injuries, if that's all right."

"That's fide, Duke."

Mary opened the handbag, revealing one and three-quarters bread rolls. A few crumbs were visible on the white napkin next to the shy but now well-fed Tycho. The Duke slowly reached into the bag and gently cradled Tycho in his large hands, rough and thick for a man of royalty. He brought him out and turned him about, gently examining the injured raven spirit.

"Let me have a look at your head there. You suffered a nasty blow, haven't you?" The Duke's eyes conveyed great kindness. Something about the way Duke Václav's hooded eyelids sloped always added to his kind expression. After examining Tycho from all angles, he said, "I have just the right thing for you, Tycho. Wait here, I shall return shortly."

Duke Václav left the room, and his hovering guards followed him out, leaving them alone in the vast ballroom. Mary looked at her mentor the eel, and she couldn't help but convey the pain and stress she had been going through over abandoning Darkhorse and failing to help Luis. The eel smiled, and quiet music suddenly seemed to transmit from the ether.

"Are you making that music?" Mary asked.

Without answering, Aal hovered over to her. "May I have this dance?"

Mary nodded and smiled as best she could as she held out

her arm. They twirled around the room joyously waltzing as Tycho giggled. After a few moments the doors opened, and Aal stopped the music. Like good dance partners, they both moved swiftly to their original positions next to the table as two guards entered, likely aware of their feeble attempts to give the impression they had been casually standing there the whole time – certainly not galloping around the room to magically transmitted music only they could hear.

The Duke entered with a soft red velvet pillow, upon which rested a cone-shaped piece of ornate gold jewelry in the same shape and size as Tycho's now-lost living beak.

"Tycho, this is a very special piece." With a great deal of excitement, the Duke spoke softly, the sound of his voice reverberated throughout the large empty room. The *S* and *T* sounds particularly hissed with great emphasis.

"Taken from the original Royal Orb of Bohemia, this is a royal artifact which was, and still is, a key component of our royal crown jewels. The original orb, replaced long ago, mysteriously went missing for several centuries. The dead realm has taken possession of certain artifacts, various relics and jewels. I have the distinct honor of crafting these materials into charms. Being designated to aid only those most deserving of their powers is a majestic and solemn duty."

The Duke's articulate voice was mesmerizing, and the raven gazed intently as he continued, "We've divided the orb into several charms, and this one..." He held up something shiny. "Tycho, this one I crafted myself right here in Prague Castle a few months ago. It was then sent off to the sages of Edinburgh for enchantment, under a full moon, on the night of spring equinox. Therefore, the golden charm dubbed The Neb of Ostara is for use by a special individual."

"An individual like me?" Tycho thought with great hope.

"Yes, you have been deemed worthy of an enhanced afterlife, which will be realized, thanks in part to the abilities this endows. I subconsciously made this especially for you," the Duke said.

With a little effort, the Duke slowly guided the broad end of the ornate golden artifact toward the shattered bill of Tycho. Closing his eyes and whispering unintelligible words, loose pieces of shattered organic matter and dried blood split away from the bird's head, disintegrating out of existence. As if magnetic, the bejeweled beak fastened snugly and comfortably on Tycho's head. It looked impossibly as if it had always been there. Tycho blinked his eyes a few times and Duke Václav held up a small mirror.

"Tycho, what do you think?" he asked.

Tycho seemed transfixed by the appearance of a handsome and mystical raven in the mirror – and rightly so. He looked to Mary and Aal, then back at the mirror, speechless.

He seemed to hesitate to speak for a moment before finally saying, "I am honored." His voice nearly had the tenor and diction of a radio announcer. Mary smiled at Tycho's lyrical new voice, and Tycho continued, "Thank you so much for this most gracious gift."

"Isn't that something?" Aal said.

Mary was speechless. The transformation was truly astounding.

"The Neb of Ostara endows you with many abilities, Tycho. Not just this new voice. The most powerful is levitation. Thanks to this new golden bill, whatever you carry in your beak or claws will defy gravity as you grip it. You can hoist almost anything; the most gargantuan mass would be as light as a feather as long as you can grasp it or something attached to it."

"Really!?" Tycho asked.

"You could carry an elephant by the tail or tow a registered accountant by his briefcase," Aal replied.

After a short debriefing, they all thanked Duke Václav and exited the castle to return to Amsterdam. Passing back out through the gates of the palace, Aal noted the Bohemian sun had finally found a clearing through the clouds. Mary, Aal and Tycho made their way down the hill and across the bridge toward the station.

"Mary, the midday is lovely, and I'd be delighted to see you at least partially over the bridge before diving back into the water."

"Excellent," she replied, and together they made their way down to the bridge back through the curvy streets of cafés and shops.

Between jubilant sorties patrolling high overhead and exploring the views of the city, Tycho returned to perch comfortably on Mary's shoulder. He'd lean his head with its glimmering beak upon her warm neck, and his charcoal eyelids pinched out tiny tears of gratitude. Tycho had clearly bonded to her, and Mary was grateful to have catered a successful arrival for the raven, so far.

"I'm going to go explore some more. I'll be right back," Tycho exclaimed before disappearing far across the river to the east.

Tycho's perseverance through the terrible anguish and fear relieved Mary. She knew he would be an excellent addition to the house in Amsterdam but worried perhaps the house might not be in order enough to serve him.

"What a remarkable transformation. Well done, Mary," Aal said.

"Thank you, Aal. I've needed a success like this. I need to tell you about what happened on the train. I feel terrible about it."

Mary went into all the details she could recall about the incident with the Soul Reaper and Luis.

"I am to blame for that bartender's condition. I am a guardian. I should have done more to protect the people on that train."

"Mary, you did the best you could. The thing came out of the blue. You cannot blame yourself for not recognizing the extent of the threat. Even though the experience was tragic, now you can anticipate such situations in the future."

After a few minutes, Tycho returned hoisting a massive bronze statue in his claws. The sun reflected softly off his golden etched beak as he fluttered, placing the monument down in front of them on the bridge. Freestanding and apparently not bolted down, it was perhaps assumed by its installers to remain safely held in place due to its enormous mass.

"Look what I found! He has two eye patches just like the badger in the cathedral tower!"

Aal said the statue was that of the legendary Czech general Jan Žižka.

"Oh Tycho! Listen darling, it is fantastic that you are getting practice with your new ability, but you need to learn to be more discreet with your new powers. Be more respectful of the monuments to the dead. Please do me a favor and put it back carefully, just the way you found it."

"Oh, sure, I can do that," the innocent raven replied and towed the massive monument back over the river into the distance.

"He'll learn his boundaries soon enough, Mary. Your patience with the newly dead is one of the traits that makes you such an excellent guardian."

Aal excused himself to return through his portal to Amsterdam for lunch with Darkhorse and Gerald. He dove into the water and disappeared into its dark, chilly depths.

10

I n Amsterdam, Darkhorse and Gerald were making their way to one of the many small cafés featuring the nearly identical veranda layouts, for what Aal referred to as "dining air-fresco". On the sunny south side of the *Singelgracht* canal, at one of several bridges, cafés appeared almost identical. Something about this layout made these cafés particularly popular, which explained their ubiquity, and if one was too full, another was just up the way.

As Gerald and Darkhorse made their way up the canal, the dead horse revealed an introspective mood. He was always quiet, so there wasn't much unusual for Gerald to notice, and he too was deep in thought about his situation in the afterlife.

After Darkhorse's fall into the canal and Aal's rescue, he had emerged from a dark place and now had a new perspective on his last session with Mary. When he revealed his feelings of resentment for Gerald, Mary pointed out that Gerald was a good friend, and that he should feel happy for him for graduating to the next phase of existence. Darkhorse realized that since Gerald would be gone forever in a few days, he should create pleasant memories with Gerald by accepting and celebrating his friend's success rather than ruminating on his own lack of progress. Maybe, Darkhorse reasoned, he was a bit too preoccupied with himself.

The pair approached the café, and Gerald took a seat at the familiar spot near the water.

"I will miss these beer and snack sessions with you guys," Gerald said, boisterously.

Darkhorse sauntered to the table and sat down. "Ja, me too," he replied.

They gazed at the laminated menus despite knowing them well and would likely order the same things they always did. Darkhorse watched birds fly playfully over the canal, debating whether he should confront Gerald about his imminent abandonment of his friends.

"Back at the house there is a great deal of anticipation for Mary's return," Gerald said.

"Yep, she holds the house together – or tries to anyway."

"Indeed, she does." Gerald agreed, put down the well-worn, familiar menu and looked at Darkhorse. "Mary is doing a great job, don't you think?"

"Well, I guess. So, this is our last borrel?" said Darkhorse, not-so-subtly ignoring the question.

"Indeed, Darkhorse. I tell you, I'm beginning to get sentimental about everything."

"Oh, cold feet?"

"No, I'm determined to go, but I am really trying to experience this afterlife process by being in the present and relishing every step toward departure. I love you all, but to graduate properly requires a certain level of detachment," Gerald said.

"Detachment. Must be nice to just block your emotions," replied Darkhorse.

"Darkhorse, are you enjoying your afterlife?"

"Not really. Frankly, I am starting to think that it mostly sucks."

"Oh, my friend, you should do more to focus on the positive. There are so many joys to experience. Keep talking to Mary. She is well equipped to help you, an amazing individual – probably one in ten billion."

"Easy for you to say, you are about ready to graduate."

"Reaching your destination is quicker and less burdensome if you find ways to appreciate the journey. Enjoy the present, it won't last forever."

Darkhorse had an urge to burst out, to complain about the cursed bindings he faced daily. But when he looked at Gerald, he felt renewed compassion for him. What was left of the rhino's horns – crudely shorn, stubby platforms – reminded Darkhorse that Gerald too had endured an afterlife filled with pain, grief, and indignities. He was equally justified to resent his fate but no longer did.

"Yes, I should, there is really no other choice. I am just going through a really rough patch."

"You are doing fine; everything has its time and purpose. I have seen you make great strides. Remember how you were when you first got here?"

Darkhorse thought about it and realized that not that long ago, he couldn't even leave his room, let alone travel to a café. Gerald's encouragement made him feel better, but appreciating Gerald triggered shame for the fleeting feelings of resentment he held against him, just below the surface.

"Oh, there he is!" Gerald smiled and pointed to Aal's pale body winding just below the murky canal's surface. He swam toward them, disappearing behind the ledge for a moment, then emerged up from the side, slithered between parked bikes, and started across the shaded flagstone. He dodged a pair of bicycles and left behind a trail of water. Glistening in the sun, he took a seat at the table.

"Gentlemen, is there room for this thirsty old eel to join you?"

Unlike Darkhorse and Aal, who had been at the house for well over a century, Gerald had been in the afterlife for a few decades since his deadly encounter with ivory poachers. Darkhorse still questioned if it really was the right time for him to depart the afterlife, but who was he to decide?

Nearby, the dead waiter placed two small beers and a bowl of peanuts before a table of otters. He then twirled the serving tray under his arm, strode over and greeted Darkhorse's familiar group. Aal ordered a large bowl of "bitterballen" for the table and a small pilsner for himself. Without hesitation Gerald added the same beer to the order for himself, but "Super Groot" (Extra Large). Finally, Darkhorse ordered his staple beverage, Fanta.

"Any news about the new housemate?" asked Gerald.

"Oh, yes. In fact, I was just speaking with him," said Aal. "Quite a remarkable raven, and they have bestowed him with an enchanted prosthetic treasure to replace his shattered beak. He will fit in well, and I suspect he will enable a great deal of fresh excitement."

"Wonderful," the rhino exclaimed.

"And how is Mary?" Darkhorse asked.

"Mary is fine. They were on their way to the train station when I left. She should be home late this afternoon."

The three old friends gazed for a few moments out onto the canal at soaring pigeons and seagulls in a state of playful aerial dogfighting.

"I wonder if I was ever a bird?" pondered Gerald. "What a marvelous sensation it must be to glide through the air like that."

"I heard once that flying is painful to birds, that it requires them to strain and tear their chest muscles in order to maintain the flapping speed to stay airborne. What looks to some like a blessing is, actually, a curse," Darkhorse replied.

Neither Gerald or Aal chose to say anything, given Darkhorse's prickly mood.

"You know, I want to tell you both something," Gerald said. "My greatest success in death has come thanks to you guys. I mean the whole house, yes, but you two especially. I am so grateful to you two. You have both helped me develop a broader perspective on the universe and existence. It is thanks to you and Mary that I have learned to appreciate and celebrate how different we all are. It took many years, but I have finally found a way to be happy with who I am. I don't need my horns to feel complete. But what I do need is you – my friends. Accepting such a simple concept wholeheartedly is surprisingly freeing, and it has been the key to my success. I am so grateful for your support of my graduation."

"So, what you learned is that what matters most are us, your friends. With this lesson, now you are ready to leave us?" Darkhorse said.

"Ha! Yes, I know it seems contradictory. You have taught me to accept myself for who I am. That freed me from my anxiety and has empowered me. I have grown comfortable enough to welcome friends into my life, and your acceptance has taught me to accept myself. I've learned that confidence builds confidence, and it is essential to maintain healthy relationships. You are great friends, and you have played a great role in my happiness."

"Well said," replied Aal.

"Okay, I think I get it." Darkhorse nodded. Inside he was embarrassed that he still felt a mixture of admiration and envy.

Then the molten, steamy bitterballen arrived – seasoned mashed potatoes rolled into spheres about the size of a golf ball, covered with Panko batter and deep fried until golden brown.

Gerald held one up. "The king of Dutch fried food. Delicious, savory and washes down well with a cold beer."

The three enjoyed tucking away the hot, crispy contents of the large bowl. In the past Aal had stated a strategy for dining on bitterballen. The key was to start slow, crack a crusty dome off the top of the sphere so the steam could escape and utilize the cool mustard to reduce the lava-like aspects of the tasty interior. Each subsequent treat would cool more, and it was important not to order so many that the last few got to room temperature before you got to them.

Both living and dead bicyclists breezed by, as did the occasional motor scooter Darkhorse found a bit annoying. He contemplated whether to mention that it was his Deathday.

"Who wants the last bitterball?" Gerald asked.

"You have it, my friend, I am stuffed," said Aal.

"Yes, I am stuffed too." Darkhorse leaned back in his seat, satisfied by the warm feeling in his belly.

Gerald tossed the last warm bitterball high in the air, flicking a few strays of crispy fried crumbs overhead, and his enormous mouth opened wide. The dense snack landed in the center of his open jaws, and he chomped down, mashing the savory, herb-seasoned potato treat between his tongue and the roof of his mouth. He followed it with half a pint of beer, its suds rinsing the sticky umami flavor down the back of his broad throat. He let out a massive belch, echoing up and down the canal, rousing birds who were perched in a tree across the way. His mouth closed into a broad smile, and his nostrils unleashed a rushing sigh of satisfaction.

"Well, that is the belch of a truly free soul," Aal said, and he chuckled.

Darkhorse, usually entertained by such behavior, didn't react. "Some of us will miss you a whole lot," he said.

"I know. I love being with you all, and I have tried to make the most of every moment in the afterlife. I have grown so fond of all my friends here, but it is right for me to go now."

"What about Fawn? Is it right for her? Did you even consider her needs amid your great enlightenment?" Darkhorse had never expressed such direct aggression to Gerald before.

They sat in silence for a moment. The eel and rhinoceros were in no rush to react. Gerald did not jump into a defensive state, and Aal did not feel the need to refute Darkhorse's accusation of callousness.

"All realm transitions, from life to afterlife, or from the afterlife to beyond, are often more painful for those who try to hold onto the individual, rather than letting them go," said the rhino.

Darkhorse began to cry. "I will miss you."

The mystical eel smiled. "We will have fond memories of you, Gerald. Your spirit will forever echo from the hearts of those you've impacted. We are never completely separated; if we look and listen, we can enjoy glimpses of those we've lost."

"Now you are talking way over my head," remarked Darkhorse.

"Sorry, my friend," Aal said.

Gerald concluded Aal's statement with this thought: "Darkhorse, nothing lasts forever. We should be in the present moments together and celebrate connections we have, rather than dreading our separation. Enjoying the moment is what life is all about."

"Then I want another orange soda," said Darkhorse.

11

M ary continued to the station back in Prague, crossing the Charles Bridge. The early morning fog had completely burned off and only a few clouds speckled the sky. Some tourists populated the bridge as Mary enjoyed her stroll. She hoped Tycho was dutifully replacing the statue as she requested, and equally that he would return without another priceless monument in tow. She planned what words would resonate with Tycho. She didn't want to quash the joyful whimsy at the core of his character, but he needed to be more mindful of the responsibilities inherent in using the afterlife powers he had been endowed.

A wisp of smoke wafted by, perhaps from an exotic-meats sausage vendor. But it soon grew thick, then surrounded her. When she recognized the smell, a jarring charge of dread shot through her. She turned around and was blasted directly toward her face with a mass of the Soul Reaper's black soot. She dodged, but still a liberal dose of the toxic plume entered her nostrils, and with painful stinging in her eyes, she doubled over.

She took hold of her talisman pendant and, in defense, triggered a strong percussive blast of energy out from her core. The black swirl that accompanied the creature blew into dust at just the moment when the creature was attempting to grip her by the neck and wrists. Bystander spirits on the bridge fell to the stone ground before rising and scampering away. Mary coughed and coughed, covering her face with her sleeve as she waited desperately for her talisman to recharge.

The effects of the fumes tasted and smelled awful, like boiling tar. The putrid odor was backed by an inescapable sulfur smell, the kind that would linger on clothing for a long time. The mist enveloped her again, and she tried to step away, wanting desperately to get to safety. Surrounded by a swirl of gloomy mist, she staggered to the edge of the bridge. Her knees weakened, and she grabbed the bridge guardrail for support. She felt overwhelming nausea and pain deep in her core. It swirled through her organs like cuts from a blade.

Her vulnerability in the face of something so relentlessly wicked was deeply familiar. Her talisman glowed, indicating it was ready, but as she tried to grip it with her fingers, her muscles were so convulsed that the pendant tumbled out of her grip and her handbag fell from her shoulder, though its straps caught on the inside of her elbow. Her leg muscles seized up, and she fell to the ground. There was no way her contorted fingers could close properly, and now with her legs unable to keep her standing, she felt almost completely helpless. Spasms rippled through her body, and she convulsed, uncontrollably on the stone bridge as the monster approached, looming over her.

For the first time in the afterlife, Mary felt absolute terror and deep dread. She had the horrifying thought that if she wound up like Luis, she'd never see her Tragically Dead friends recover; her afterlife's mission would be cut short.

A sooty vapor spread, she couldn't see beyond its opaque mist, and to protect herself from more exposure, she held her breath, closed her eyes, rolled over onto her stomach so that she could grip the pendant with her lips. With clenched teeth, she held the talisman, positioning it in her mouth enough to activate it and form a levitation field, hoisting herself upon the thick stone ledge of the bridge's guardrail. The coughed uncontrollably and had to release the pendant from her lips.

The beast approached, extended his skeletal fingers and roared like a wild, injured animal. Through the scream, she heard a distinct voice say, "Mary, please help me." It was familiar, but she had no time to ponder on it. More spasms rippled through the tension of her coiled muscles and gnarled hands. Her mind raced for a strategy, wishing she had the dexterity to properly grasp her pendant and simply vanquish the monster once and for all. But the situation was desperate. The best she could hope for was to retreat, and given her incapacitation, the only way to put great distance between her and the creature, was to roll over and let herself fall into the river. She'd be unlikely to manage to swim with the muscle convulsions, so would experience perpetual drowning – a fate befitting her, due to the failure to save Luis from a similar fate on the train.

The monster lunged forward. Its clawed hands reached out to her, and she closed her eyes again, just managing to shift her weight away and begin to tip off the ledge, and plunge into the cold water. Yet frustratingly, she didn't fall. A gentle tug suspended her for a moment. Had it grabbed her? She felt a refreshing breeze of fresh air, and just barely opened her eyes. She wasn't falling, she was ascending. Mary realized she was suddenly high above the bridge and gasped, inhaling the refreshing clear air. She began to clear her airways from the fumes she had inhaled. Her chest felt inflamed and sandy, she coughed uncontrollably then managed to open tear-filled eyes. It was Tycho towing her, via the handle of her bag.

Mary felt no physical strain gripping the bag thanks to the transmission of the gravity-defying ability of the raven's charmed neb. Her weight was no burden to her or Tycho, who soared swiftly above the city. She saw in the distance below a tiny black path of puff, racing furiously back and forth along the edge of the bridge, unable to pursue them. Far out of danger from the monster, together Mary and Tycho ascended high into the clouds.

"Mary, what was that thing?"

"I don't know, Tycho." Mary could barely speak between coughs – uncontrollable for a long time.

Tycho glided high above Prague, circling safely away from the creature and exposing Mary to the freshest air he could find. Traumatized by the encounter with the Soul Reaper, he said he was too afraid to land.

"Should I take you back to the Duke? Or to Jerome?" he asked.

"No, we must get to the train station." Her voice quivered, and she continued coughing.

She must not have been exposed to as much of the ghastly plume as Luis was, because thankfully, she could speak and breathe between coughs. She shut her eyes, barely holding onto consciousness.

"Rest, sweet Mary, I'll take care of you now," he said.

She'd survived the encounter with the creature and lost consciousness, blacking out for the next several hours. She finally awoke lying on a bench on the station platform, being protected by Tycho, who wouldn't let any spirit share the bench with his vulnerable guardian. The newly arrived but clever bird had figured out what platform the afterlife train to Amsterdam would depart from, and he nudged her awake just in time to board. With a gentle tug from his beak, he helped her stand, and gingerly, the two found Mary's private cabin.

He let her down softly onto her cushion and cracked open the window. She was grateful, the fresh air would do her good; she still had a horrific cough. Then he covered her with a travel blanket, unbuckled and slipped off her shoes, and doted on her in every way he could, bringing cold water and helping her find various elixirs in her handbag to aid in her recovery.

In time, Mary recovered enough to sit up. "Tycho, what a wonderful bird you are."

"You're welcome, Mary. Do you feel better?"

"Yes, I am still weak, and my throat is sore, but feeling a bit better." Her voice croaked, and she held her handkerchief up to her mouth. Through the carriage window she looked at the platform clock. It was evening, and they were supposed to have arrived in Amsterdam an hour ago. She summoned a messenger orb and sent word to Aal that they would arrive in the morning but left out the details of why. For now, she could rest, there was a doctor near Amsterdam station who might be able to find her something for her dreadful cough.

She looked at her reflection in the glass. Her eyes were watery and red, and dark rings hung under her lashes. She was overcome with exhaustion from all that had transpired that day. She sobbed covertly, feeling sincere gratitude for her newest friend.

After the halfway mark, Mary managed to sit up comfortably, and Tycho perched on her knee the whole way back. When they returned to Amsterdam Central Station, Mary visited the office of her friend Dr. Mahal, but he was nowhere to be found. She coughed into her handkerchief and decided that they ought to take the scenic canal route home. It was less effort than a stroll, took about the same amount of time, and would be a nice introduction of the canal district to Tycho.

Mary and Tycho approached a long, wide, flat tour boat. They boarded near the bow, just as the door was closing. They passed through the center aisle flanked by padded seats and tables where the living ticket holders were seated. The arch of windows afforded clear views of the canals and buildings alongside it. The boat was drifting from its mooring. Tycho had to duck as Mary made her way through the interior of the vessel. Despite Mary's uncontrollable coughs, the human shapes were oblivious to the presence of the two stowaway spirits.

Mary then emerged with Tycho undetected onto the open and unoccupied stern of the boat. The morning breeze and the subtle sea smells from the canal welcomed Mary home. They sat at the end near the motor, and she felt comforted by the gentle bob as its gurgling secondary thrusters rotated the vessel.

The motor roared gently, barely audible in the afterlife, leaving behind a foamy wake as it headed west toward *Prinsengracht*. She thought about the noise of the Soul Reaper's roars. Why did the monster seek her out specifically for help? And if it needed help, why had it attacked her? She couldn't wait to talk to Aal about this.

Mary wasted no time filling Tycho's capable afterlife mind with her breadth of knowledge about Amsterdam. She pointed out some of the details of the canal district as a way of introducing him to a brief history of the so-called "Golden Age" and the root of its existence: the formation of the Dutch East India Company (Verenigde Oost-Indische Compagnie or VOC). The VOC's exploits enriched investors and merchants in the seventeenth century, which spurred the growth leading to the ornate and monumental system of canal houses. Their narrow and tall designs were due to the method of taxation at the time of their construction, based in large part upon their width. Quaint bridges crossing the canals, decked out with fresh flowers, were full of parked bikes along the railings.

Tycho said he was surprised to hear that the boats on either side of the canal housed human inhabitants. He noted the numerous Amsterdammers and tourists lounging upon the water's edges relaxing, eating, drinking, smoking, and/or chatting merrily.

"Dead Amsterdammers seem so happy and carefree compared to the living."

"When you are dead, all you have is your essence. It forces us to set the trivialities aside."

She pulled out a map of central Amsterdam to show Tycho where they were and where home was.

"We are just where the horseshoe shape of *Herengracht* starts to turn here." She pointed as another uncontrollable cough took her over, and she folded up the map and put it away.

THE *WESTERTOREN*, the tower of *Westerkerk* came into view as they rounded a bend, topped with a large blue globe and crown, a burgundy-colored clockface halfway down. And as if on cue, it began ringing out a melody.

"The blue orb looks like the seas on the globe in Jerome's study."

"Yes, it does, doesn't it? You know, when I was a girl in the living realm, I spent many hours gazing upon that tower through my window. Back then the orb was painted golden."

For a moment, Mary went into a daze of personal nostalgia at the sight of West Church. She thought again of Peter. The boat edged into place. Gentle intermittent blasts from its side thrusters slowly positioned the boat to kiss the side of the canal. She assured him that the familiar bell could also be heard from the house of the Tragically Dead in Recovery, so he would have many opportunities to learn its different melodies.

"Great! I can't wait to hear what all it has." The raven didn't mean to be so crude when he then blurted out, "Hey Mary, where did you die?"

"I died very far away. I lived, and I loved. Though, I had to hide."

"Who did you love?"

"I loved my family and my friends."

"Yeah but who did you *love* love?"

"That's an awfully personal question, Tycho, but seeing as how you just saved my life, I will divulge this, but keep it to yourself. His name was Peter."

"Peter. Did Peter love you too?"

"I think he loved me very much. We have long been apart. He is still among the living. I focus on the Tragically Dead now. You are my only priority." She smiled warmly but then was taken by her cough.

12

The boat docked, but Mary stayed seated as most of the living stood up and crowded the front.

"Why don't we just pass through the living forms and get moving?" Tycho asked.

"It is considered impolite unless absolutely necessary or unavoidable. When the dead intersect with the living, it gives us both terrible chills."

Once the last few living shapes were about to exit, Mary stood and strolled just behind the last tourist to depart. Although she followed closely, she avoided intersecting with the shadowy, jittery form. Then once they were on land, Mary avoided passing through the line of living queued up to enter the boat, walking along the edge of the canal.

As they walked east, past *Westerkerk* (West Church) and made their way south toward the house, Tycho said, "Mary, I'll be right back. I want to get a quick bird's-eye view of the neighborhood to match it to the map you showed me."

"Okay, please don't pick up *anything!*" she shouted with a nervous smile as he soared high above. Mary was happy to be back home, but then she wondered if Darkhorse was all right, feeling guilty that she'd forgotten to even ask Aal about him when Aal met her in Prague.

Tycho returned to Mary, thankfully with nothing in his bill – not an Albert Heijn grocery delivery vehicle, nor the sculpture of Atlas atop the old royal palace, nor the old VOC ship that sat at the harbor behind the Maritime Museum. He perched on her shoulder and began his excited report and inquiry of all the things he saw. Then he said, "...and Mary, I see, so the canals are laid out like concentric horseshoes, with spokes emanating. From the center, just like the map you showed me."

"Yes, and your new home is on the second canal band from the center, *Herengracht.*"

"Here-in-graaaaaw?" The last part he crowed.

"Close enough." Mary smiled.

"So do people live in all of these boats in the big canals all year?"

"The bigger enclosed ones are usually occupied all year, but the smaller ones, or ones that are open, are just for occasional excursions."

"What a cool place. I think I will love it here!"

"Good, I know you will, and you will be able to visit countless other cities across the continent."

"Sounds fun!"

"You are going to be a great addition to the house, Tycho, and they are all excited to meet you, I'm sure."

BACK AT THE HOUSE, Aal was helping ensure that the preparations for Tycho's heralded arrival would be ready. He had checked in with the longtime residents, the frozen birds. They were warmly anticipating the appearance of a new feathered friend.

Fawn, the house's informal art director, created a quaint rendering of what she assumed Tycho would look like from Aal's description. She used blues and blacks for his body, and orange and yellow to approximate the golden bill Aal described. She plopped the inky brush from her mouth into a jar of water to rinse and summoned the eel.

"Aal, come look, is this what Tycho looks like?"

"Excellent, Fawn! A wonderful rendition of our new friend." Aal offered encouragement to the artistic little doe. Her inky drawing was charming, and crude enough to present an inoffensive approximation of Tycho and his golden bill.

"Nailed it!" she exclaimed and took her jars of paint to the kitchen sink, prancing down the hall, spilling only a few drops of ink on the runner in the hallway.

Gerald held up the just-dried banner, and a set of mice

climbed up his body with fasteners in their mouths. They twisted the tacks through the cloth and into the wall until the banner was hung over the wide entryway into the main room. Then they rolled it up to be unfurled at Tycho's imminent arrival.

"Tres bien!" Aal replied.

With great anticipation, everyone gathered in the main room. A full tea was prepared and just about ready. Dominic the fox, who was polishing his coins in the sunlight, suddenly announced from the windowsill that Mary and Tycho were in sight. He gently closed his jar of coins and returned them to a hidden panel nook for safe keeping just before several of the dead stampeded to the windows to catch a preview of the newest resident. They were in awe of Tycho's golden beak. It glimmered and shone even from a great distance.

Mary entered the house, glided up the steps and walked into the main room, crammed with all the Tragically Dead in Recovery. They held their breath, waiting patiently for Mary to speak.

"Everyone, meet our newest member, Tycho!"

The room burst into loud cheers and applause. The banner was unfurled, and Mary smiled at its charm: "Welkom Thuis Tycho!" it read, and to the right of the text was Fawn's illustration.

"Look at this amazing welcome banner you all made! How thoughtful!"

Tycho stood a bit stiffly, his claws clutching tightly to Mary. A large group of Tragically Dead could be intimidating at first glance. Some more than others.

The little doe trotted up first and said assertively, "Hi, I'm Fawn. I'm the boss around here, so get used to it."

The doe trotted off, and Tycho looked up to Mary. She scrunched her lips and subtly shook her head to indicate that he needn't take the doe's assertion seriously. Others approached and welcomed him graciously. Some took a moment to indicate briefly how they'd died, as this was still a strong component of their self-identity. The only one Mary had to cut off was the chronically frazzled swan, who as usual went on and on about aviation congestion and "the dangers of the jet age." He even tried to present Tycho with a pamphlet, but Mary declined it, politely reminding him that this was a welcome party. She brought Tycho toward the fireplace. She was fatigued and leaned on the mantel shelf while the frozen birds welcomed Tycho and showcased their arrangements on the hearth alongside the mice.

Gerald stepped into the center of the room and held up a stubby armored finger to signal he wanted to speak.

"Hey everyone, while you are all here, I've been having conversations with Aal, and Darkhorse, and Mary of course, and they all know what I am about to say." He smiled at Mary, and she nodded. The group fell into a somber hush as if they knew what he was about to say.

"It has been over thirty-seven years since I was poached for my ivory. I have dealt with this trauma, and I now refuse to let my death define me. Thanks to Mary, Aal, and many of you – I have met the most amazing friends to support and guide me through the afterlife. I love you all, and it would be great to get to know Tycho more, but I feel that I have made all the progress I need to in the afterlife. I have decided that I am ready to take the next step in my journey. The time is right for me to grad-uate and leave the afterlife realm."

Understandably, the announcement fostered reactions that reflected mixed emotions. But after a few seconds, a burst of cheers rang out, followed by a flurry of congratulations from his friends – well most, anyway. The outraged doe tearfully broke up the celebration by letting out a loud street whistle from her cloven hoof, demanding the room's attention. For a few seconds she glared defiantly at Gerald, both standing in the center of the room.

"You talked to everyone that matters, huh? Darkhorse, Aal and Mary. Well, what about your best friend?"

Gerald cocked his head to the side and stepped timidly toward her. "Fawn, I –"

The doe cut him off. "No, Gerald! You had all kinds of opportunities to tell me. Mary, you always say that the afterlife gives us what we want. Well, I don't want Gerald to leave!" Tears ran down Fawn's furry face.

Mary was exhausted, but wanted to calm the situation down and comfort Fawn. Cut to the bone from the encounter on the bridge, she was far from her peak state to contend with this emotional crisis. She gathered her thoughts and prepared to say something, but could only hold in her aching cough.

Standing on her hind hooves with front ones on her hips, the outraged little doe continued taking out her frustration on...well, just about everyone and everything.

"The afterlife is a stupid sham. Why don't most of us get any magical stuff? This newbie raven got a fricking golden beak and he's been here what, two days?"

Tycho looked down at the ground.

Mary couldn't let the doe continue to vent; this outburst was now causing real emotional damage.

"Faw –" She started to speak, but her hoarse throat clinched, and again a dreadful coughing fit took her over.

Aal sat upright with a look of concern. Mary was clearly not well.

Fawn continued, "Sorry, Tycho, I'm sure you're cool and all. I'm happy for you I guess, but you'll see eventually that this place is a joke! You die, then when you find a best friend, they leave!"

Aal spoke up. "Mary, if I may say something?"

Mary nodded as she held her handkerchief to her mouth.

"Fawn," he continued, "what you are feeling is completely valid, and you are not alone. I know this hurts you especially. Gerald is a fantastic friend, and he loves you very much, but part of maturing is understanding that good things come, and they must eventually go."

Mary regained her voice and added, "Fawn, it seems terribly unfair, but this is the rhythm of existence. The great sense of loss from his departure is directly proportionate to the value –" she was cut off by an uncontrollable cough.

Aal completed the thought. "The truth is, everything must eventually balance itself out. The universe distributes joy and sorrow like waves. Some large, some small, but bliss and pain ebb and flow in equal measure. If you cherish the experiences and memories of Gerald, in that way, he will forever not just be with you, but even better, he will remain a part of you."

Fawn rolled her tear-filled eyes and stormed out of the room, scampering down the stairs in an awkward hurry.

The room was shocked, overwhelmed by the emotions. But Helma, one of the frozen birds, went to the window and relayed her position like a play-by-play radio correspondent. "She's on the street, heading south along the canal. She stopped now. *Oké*, she's turning around. Some guy is approaching her carrying a bunch of notebooks." A few gasped at the development. "Oh no, you have no idea what you are getting into, guy. Oh, she turned back around. She's rearing up. She kicked him. Oh, papers are flying everywhere. Now she's heading down the alley toward the center of the city." Helma turned to Mary. "She's out of sight. Should we follow her?"

"No, it's fine. She can handle herself. Let's just give her some time to –" Mary coughed. "...cool off."

The Tragically Dead carried on as best they could with the celebration, though less enthusiastically. They had two good reasons to celebrate, but at least one reason to worry. Several congratulated the raven for his arrival. A few asked if they could touch his new beak. A trio of otters made plans for Gerald's graduation event. As tradition had established, the departure of a member of the household to the next level of existence had developed with efficiency into a going away party and magical ritual, all in one.

Aal slithered over to check on Mary. "Mary, what is this cough? Are you all right?"

"Yes, but I need to talk to you."

"Of course. By the way, I am sure that Fawn will be fine. She is very attached to Gerald."

The two talked as they made their way past the astonished cluster surrounding Tycho as the raven lifted the heavy tortoise off the ground.

Mary spoke in a hushed tone to her mentor, Aal. "I just wish Fawn wouldn't take things out on others, especially poor Tycho. It's his first day here."

A set of Fawn's little mouse admirers approached with furrowed brows. One said, "Mary, can we go look for Fawn?"

"Sure, that's fine. Just try to be back before dark, so we don't worry."

They agreed and scampered off down the stairs and out while Aal followed Mary up to her attic suite and sat down in her well-appointed counselor's parlor.

13

In Mary's attic suite, she began to describe both encounters with the Soul Reaper to Aal. Between coughs she described the encounter on the train and told of Luis's harrowingly debilitating condition.

"Before you go on any further," Aal said, "allow me to heal you. I will only need to make contact through the outside of your neck, and it will only take a few seconds. With your permission of course."

"Yes, Aal, please do whatever you need to," Mary consented.

Long ago he had told Mary that he had powers to take on disease and afflictions like a sponge. He could absorb almost any ailment and take on the burden of the affliction, but he would then need to heal himself by swimming through a portal to any of the several healing waters of the world.

"Just try to relax." The mystical eel hovered onto her shoulder and wrapped his long pale body around her neck like a kindly boa.

He closed his eyes, and Mary glanced at their reflection in the mirror above the fireplace. She could see his body was taking on dark moving shapes. They swirled and churned just beneath his milky transparent skin. The tenderness and persistent itch in her throat quickly dissipated, and Aal slithered back down to the chair across from her and sat casually, looking only a bit more worn down and sickly. His almost white body was now dappled with dark spots, like ermine heraldry.

"Oh my – Thank you, Aal. I feel much better, but are you sure you'll be all right?"

She didn't want to be presumptuous but was hoping that perhaps, when the time was right, Aal would be generous enough to volunteer his powers to address the bartender's Death Cough as well.

Aal was skeptical of this possibility. "In a case as severe as his, I cannot risk taking the affliction on alone. But I may be able to collaborate with another healer to come to his aid. First, let's focus on you, dear Mary. How are you processing the trauma from these assaults?"

Mary took a breath, then went into stark detail about her encounter with the monster on the bridge, and Aal marveled at the young raven's brave rescue. Mary agreed that he had proved himself worthy of his afterlife gift, but she questioned her own.

"What haunts me is what they said to me on the train, afterward. I feel so ashamed. What kind of a guardian am I to have let that happen to that poor man? What should I have done differently?"

"You did the best you could, Mary, given the unusual encounter. A Soul Reaper stalking a dead guardian in the afterlife is perplexing." Aal paced around the arrangement of lounge chairs, occasionally looking up to the ceiling. "I have never heard of a Reaper acting this way. It is as if it has been contaminated. Perhaps it has some sort of a parasite. Something is corrupting and confusing it." He turned and looked her straight in the eye. "Mary, you must be on guard until we get to the bottom of this. Remember, Reapers can transport souls between realms. We don't want to lose you prematurely."

"Trust me, I don't want to go either. I will be fine. But most importantly, I don't want to let this thing, or the fear of it, interfere with the Tragically Dead in Recovery. I'd be impressed if it follows me all the way here to Amsterdam. Let's not worry the others. Gerald's graduation is tomorrow. It should be a celebration."

Aal still looked concerned. "It would be best if I delay my Grand Tour until the threat from the monster is eliminated, so I may stay and assist you."

"No, Aal. That is very generous, but you have delayed it long enough. I insist you go on your Grand Tour. We can't let terror and evil, no matter how menacing, detract from our afterlife joys. I insist you go."

"All right. Fine, but until my scheduled departure, I shall research the subjects of this situation and send a message to Edinburgh to inquire if any Soul Reapers have gone rogue or disappeared. I think you did the best you could under the circumstances. Be on guard always. It has attacked you twice and it wouldn't surprise me if it does indeed show up here in Amsterdam."

"I will not hesitate to be on the offense if I encounter him again."

The eel curled up slightly and coughed. "Good!" he said with a gravelly voice.

"Are you sure you shouldn't go?"

"I can hold off the symptoms and shall visit a healing well within the hour. But first, I need to fill you in on Darkhorse's Deathday morning while you were in Prague."

"Oh, yes, how did he do?" Mary had almost forgotten about abandoning Darkhorse.

"He refused my help at first. But I could see he was in a fragile state, so I swam along the canal to keep an eye on him. He tripped and shattered his jaw on the bridge railing of the bridge, then collapsed there on *Berenbrug*. It began raining, and he dragged his bones into the canal, weeping. It was awful."

Mary began to well up.

The eel continued, "After he drifted a long way down *Prinsengracht*, I swam over and offered him help again. He finally accepted it, and I escorted him safely to the Key House."

"Thank you, Aal. I am so grateful."

"Of course, Mary." The eel's voice croaked, and he let out a hard cough. "Perhaps I'd better head to a healing spring. Please give my regards to Tycho – that raven truly earned his new bill," Aal said, his voice contracted at the end of the sentence.

Mary looked concerned. "He sure saved my goose, and so did you. I must have the best friends in the afterlife. Allow me to see you out, so you can get rid of that cough." Mary walked with Aal down the stairs and out the front door.

Aal turned when he reached the edge of the canal, waved and smiled, then slithered off into the channel.

·

As the party in the main room quieted down, the Tragically Dead redistributed themselves, murmuring with concern for

Fawn's outburst. It was the primary topic of the house gossip. Mary arranged a more intimate, ad hoc afterparty. At sunset she summoned Gerald and Darkhorse to meet her canal-side at the front of the house. She explained Tycho's ability and convinced them to join her atop the roof.

"Tycho has graciously agreed to ferry us each up to the roof. We can welcome our newest member with a grand view of the Amsterdam sunset."

Darkhorse, a consummate pessimist, said, "I'll let you guys go first."

To demonstrate her faith in the skill of Tycho's new ability, Mary went first. She loaded her bike with snacks and water, then sat on the bike as if she were about to speed away along the canal. Tycho fluttered over, gripped the handlebars and pulled her and the bike right up. Mary couldn't contain a gleeful little squeal as she rose along the tree and he brought her to the roof. "Be careful to avoid the skylights. Right there is perfect," she said as she pointed past the handlebars. He placed her gently down, precisely where she'd pointed.

"Wonderful, darling. Now, go see if you can convince Darkhorse, but if he is still squeamish, we'll reassure him by bringing up Gerald."

The raven soared over the canal and dove out of Mary's sight.

On the roof, Mary was surprised to find a picnic basket and a bucket of chilled champagne with a note attached. Aal, somehow always knowing just when his unique contribution would be needed, had left a chilled bottle of fine champagne there with five glasses wrapped in napkins.

The note read:

"Let us toast to the newest member of the Tragically Dead in Recovery. Enjoy this treat from my private collection. – Aal"

"That eel," Mary said, grinning. She heard the whoosh of Tycho's wings and was delighted to see Darkhorse gradually emerge above the roofline. He was carefully hoisted by the hood of his black cloak. His dangling bones and hooves occasionally hitting like a wooden wind chime as he swayed through the air.

"Slowly, slowly," Darkhorse insisted as the raven placed him gently onto the roof.

Mary welcomed her dearest dead horse friend, and after helping him find a safe spot to sit, showed him the note Aal had left.

Finally, Gerald had Tycho tow him up by his ears, the weight of the massive rhinoceros miraculously causing no distress at all. Upon landing, he said it felt as if someone were merely tugging his ears gently.

It was a shame Aal couldn't join them, and Tycho politely insisted that their first toast be to Aal and Mary rather than he. Without them, Tycho reasoned, he wouldn't be there. The group peered across the silhouetted chimney tops and blooming trees as the sky slowly transitioned from amber to a deep orange.

Gerald reassured Tycho that Fawn's outburst was about her own problems. Darkhorse added the point that everyone at the house was on a personal journey of recovery and Tycho should feel completely worthy of his new charmed bill. Each seemed to do their best to ensure that Tycho understood he was entirely welcome. Mary was proud of her Tragically Dead.

They lounged together, leaning on one another. The late afternoon sky turned orange and magenta, and then stars appeared and the moon rose. A cool breeze whistled through the tree buds, and Mary stood up, collected the empty glasses, wrapped them back in cloth napkins and arranged them carefully into the basket. An eerie howl rang out across the city and she froze. The group was silent for a moment after the strange shriek echoed across central Amsterdam.

"Perhaps someone crossed Fawn," Gerald quipped, though

he couldn't help but feel a genuine concern for the little doe's safety. "I'll need to go looking for her if she isn't back by dawn," he said.

"That was...spooky," Darkhorse said.

The raven flew over to Mary and whispered, "What if that's the monster?"

Mary was struck with fear. What if the beast had indeed followed her to Amsterdam? She decided she should tell this group about the potential threat rather than ignore it.

"I don't want to alarm you. But since my departure for Prague, something has been stalking me. It looks like a Soul Reaper, but something is wrong with it. It emits a thick black smoke that must be avoided at all costs. If you see anything..."

"Or hear anything," Darkhorse interrupted.

Mary smiled a little. "Let me know. I can protect us, but I need you to help me guard the house and our friends."

The house's nocturnal residents – cats, rodents and bats – scampered out and up to the slanted roof. Their leader, Edgar, a bat, offered to lead a search party to identify the source of the sound.

"That'd be helpful, but please be very careful and avoid getting close to anything that looks dangerous and keep an eye out for Fawn," she said.

Edgar gave a nod of affirmation before the team dispersed far and wide throughout the city.

AFTER TYCHO dutifully returned everyone safely down, he gingerly approached Mary.

"Would it be all right if I slept in your room?"

Mary thought about it. This was not the first such request from a recently arrival. The first few nights adjusting to the afterlife were often uneasy for the Tragically Dead, and she understood that Tycho's bond with Mary was significant enough to make an exception.

"Okay, but the others will get jealous if you stay with me too many nights."

"Sure, I understand. I'm just not really sure I want to sleep out there by the fireplace," the raven said.

"You may sleep in my room tonight. But tomorrow you should try to get comfortable with the other birds."

That night the raven perched upon Mary's backboard, and the two slept soundly after a long and truly eventful day for both.

14

The decoration of the canal house was nearly complete. In the main room, streamers, balloons and bunting hung. The celebration that night would be of Gerald's time in the afterlife and to wish him farewell. A large congratulatory banner draped over the large fireplace in the main room reading: "Gefeliciteerd Gerald!" Outside, the flagpole had been retracted in order to be later mounted at an angle and extend from the second story to hold the charmingly crude effigy of the rhino, which was still under construction. In the absence of the informal house art director, the papier-mâché rendition was receiving a final coat of paint by the disembodied river otter Elmo. This was normally something Fawn would do, but there was no telling if she'd return, and he was eager to create something on his own, without the finicky doe there to nitpick his technique or aesthetics. As was the tradition, the small golden streamer reading "Geslaagd" (Dutch for "passed") would accompany the three-dimensional homage to the rhino. This had become one of several traditions at the house to celebrate a beloved member's graduation to the next realm.

Meanwhile, the "guest of honor" was out, presumably to

pick up cakes and pastries for his own celebration. But Gerald focused on something much more important to him.

He'd awakened with a cold bare belly and an ache in his heart. His friend the doe, who usually slumbered upon his tummy, left before dusk in a state of fury and sorrow. Gerald got a few hours of rest, assuming the little doe would return safely before dawn, but he found it very difficult to sleep. Finally, when it was 4:44 in the morning and she still had not returned, he couldn't resist the compulsion to go find the doe. He drafted Aal's kind help, and the two split up the work: the eel cruised the canals, and the rhino rode his bike along the streets and alleyways.

After an hour of looking, the well-connected Aal got a tip from a swan, sped through the channels and quickly found Gerald completing a loop along the south side of *Keizersgracht*. Aal bounced out of the water in front of the rhinoceros, who hit the brakes and hopped off his bike.

"Did you find her?!" Gerald asked.

"No, but I have a strong lead from a reliable source. We should focus on *Oudezijds* canal in de Wallen," the eel announced. "A swan told me he saw her there in the early morning hours."

The two raced toward the area, circling Oude Church, and then rode back north along the channel of the *Oudezijds* Achterburgwal. Upon spotting a group of swans, Aal suggested that they approach, but as they drew nearer, there was no sign of Fawn.

"Verdamme!" exclaimed Gerald, frustrated. Now he was getting very worried for the doe.

"We will find her, do not worry. I wasn't planning on leaving until after your party, and I promise, I won't leave Amsterdam until we find her," Aal said.

Gerald spotted a mass of swans floating in their direction on the canal, which at night reflected the red neon of the shops and windows.

The rhino adored the little doe. He told the eel , he was sure he couldn't bear to leave without apologizing to her. A tear ran down Gerald's cheek, and Aal was just about to offer words of comfort, when a sassy, high-pitched voice rang out from the direction of the approaching swans.

"You better apologize and have a proper goodbye!" It was the doe. She'd emerged from the white feathers of the giant swan, and her light body stood upright as she balanced, pointing one cloven hoof directly at him as the other rested her side.

"Fawn, please forgive me," begged Gerald from the edge of the path.

The swan swam toward them, and the doe hopped off and leapt into the thick arms of the kneeling rhinoceros.

"I'll forgive you. I am glad you are all 'self-actualized,'" Fawn said, waving her hooves above her head, with a dose of friendly contempt, "but I don't like that you are leaving me!"

"Well, that's a start I suppose. Would you please attend my graduation party? It won't be the same without you. I would really love for you to be there when I go. In fact, I have a special role for you, if you'd do me the honor."

"Is it what I think it is?" The doe giggled with exuberance.

Gerald chuckled, pleased that she had a change of heart. "You got it. Now I would be honored if you would join us to pick out cakes for the party."

"I'd love to," she said.

"Do you want to ride in the basket or on my shoulders?"

"Shoulders please!" she proclaimed.

The rhinoceros lifted the young spotted doe and draped her around his neck in the usual way, with her hind legs on his left shoulder, her front legs on his right. She rested her chin on the crown of his head, and the two sped away along the canal.

With a broad smile, Aal felt joyful as the wind blew past him in the basket. Together, the three friends headed to the bakery to pick out treats for the party.

After visiting the bakery, the three returned to the house, with Aal and Gerald precariously balancing stacks of bakery boxes. They arrived just in time to see the rhinoceros's charmingly crude effigy lowered into place from the flagpole. Upon seeing it, Gerald let out a big loud belly laugh, and the doe screamed with laughter.

"I'm keeping that!" she said.

Gerald parked his bike, and Aal excused himself to prepare the ceremonial passageway in the canal.

THAT AFTERNOON, before any guests arrived, Aal, Mary, and all the friends in the house congregated. Mary reminded the house that the event was a special occasion, and although there would be a mix of emotions, they should try to keep in mind that passing on from the realm is a cause for celebration. Ultimately though, there was no wrong way to feel about this, and everyone deals with the passing on of someone in their own manner.

Aal would both DJ and MC the night's events, and he put

on some lounge music to warm up the room as final preparations were made. Half the house, it seemed, got in line to sign up for karaoke. Throughout the evening, the music got louder as souls from all over the European continent arrived, so many in fact that the party quickly spilled into the street. They opened the front canal-facing windows so that the guests outside on the street could hear the music.

As the sun set, Aal introduced the first karaoke song of the night. Fawn shoved people aside and insisted she kick things off with an impassioned and befitting rendition of Wham's "Wake Me Up Before You Go-Go."

The passage on to the next and unknown phase of existence is a rare thing, one to be celebrated, and all who had ever known Gerald excitedly gathered, proud to offer their best wishes to their dear dead friend. They shared stories of his good-natured exploits in both the living and dead realms and praised his incredible progress.

Mary and Aal delivered gracious, tearful toasts, and just before midnight, rowdy toasts from several others as the setup for departure began. The main event would be the final goodbye. On the evenings of graduation at the house, the canal was specially set up to accept the graduate into the next realm. All the graduate had to do was to drink a special potion, say their last words and within seconds, they would be gone to the next phase. Traditionally a graduate would say their parting words, drink the potion and dive into the canal from the edge of the road, but as the years progressed it eventually became more customary to dive in from the nearby tree.

Teary-eyed and truly epic toasts were delivered by Mary and Aal. Darkhorse and Fawn shied away from the honor when invited. They chose to deliver more intimate tidings of farewell directly to Gerald.

As the traditional time of midnight approached, the rowdy

housemates cheerfully ushered guests to the sides of the large main room.

"Oh my, how fun!" said a tweed-jacketed zebra, delighted by the spectacle of ropes, boards, and bungee cords that were brought out of the closets. A group of tuxedoed human spirits offered their assistance, but Fawn shooed them off. She was getting even more testy than usual.

A dozen or so somewhat inebriated friends scurried to hastily set up a do-it-yourself contraption devised by Gerald. It would propel his great mammalian mass out the open front window and into the canal on a pair of skateboards. Specifically, it would be pulled through the room and away from the house by a set of eight bungee cords, pulled out the opening and connected to the large traditional hook and gable at the top of the house. It took the strength of the house's strongest fifteen creatures to pull the enormous rhinoceros back and secure him to the pipes of the kitchen sink. Truth be told, if not for Aal's discreet magic incantations, the contraption would have never worked and would have certainly destroyed the plumbing in the seventeenth-century canal house.

Aal fully faded the music and cued up the song Gerald asked to be played as he departed. With a kiss on the cheek, Mary handed Gerald the elixir that would allow him to pass into the next realm. He held up the cup proudly, and as the party, both inside and out, fell into a hush, he cleared his throat, prepared to speak his last words.

"Ladies and gentlemen, thank you all for joining me on the biggest day of my afterlife existence. It means a great deal to me that you all feel I am worthy of this gathering. I want to also thank the few members of the house who have helped me devise a unique plan for commemorating my departure."

An otter with goggles impulsively plucked the taught bungee, creating a deep bass tone. Unintentionally drawing the momentary attention of the audience, he quickly put his hands behind his back and looked down at his toes.

Gerald continued, "I want each of you to remember four things: First, you are loved. Second, you matter. Third, you should make something of yourself in a way that matters only to you. Finally, and most importantly of all, be good to one another. I will miss every one of you, but I am sure I will also see you many more times." He nodded to Aal. The Second World War–era song, "We'll Meet Again" by Vera Lynn began to play, and the entire party, inside as well as outside, sang right along.

Gerald looked at the doe, who had tears in her eyes, and whispered what would truly be his last words to her.

With Aal's precision hearing, he heard Gerald say to Fawn, "Okay, you get the honors. Send me off, sweetheart."

The little doe stepped behind him to the rope that held Gerald.

She stood in place and prepared to cut the rope, showing off by gnashing her sharp teeth in the air as the those in the room applauded while they sang, "Don't know where, don't know when..." The doe's cheeks were now becoming soaked with streams of tears from her large brown eyes.

She approached the rope and gnawed gently, almost reluctantly. After a few more seconds, the line creaked, untwisting and fraying.

With a final sharp tear of her teeth, the rope snapped, and the enormous rhinoceros launched across the room.

As he hurtled toward the open window, Gerald let out a deep, loud "Aaah!" and ducked at just the right time to pass through the rectangular opening, arcing off and landing perfectly in the center of the canal into the enchanted portal.

The splash was indeed epic. Everyone on both sides of the canal was drenched. Water reached all the way to the top story of the house, and the subsequent deep bass of celebratory house music blared louder than ever. Even neighbors in the living realm could sense the festive nature, and a few unconsciously tapped their feet with joy to the beat. The crowd of dead cheered and danced for several hours into the early morning.

Aal faded in a compilation of "Afterlife Chill," which still accommodated those who wanted to sway and hop while allowing others to cool down. He abandoned his station at the DJ booth to find Mary holding a glass of mineral water, and as the reflections of the streetlight danced in the wavy murk, her feet rested over the concrete ledge of the canal.

"Well, graduations never get old, do they?" Aal said.

"Certainly, and that is one we will be sure to remember... for a long time." Mary's voice quivered just slightly as she finished her sentence.

Every graduation was an emotional event for her since she'd built deep bonds with every individual at the house, but more than tears for the departure, they were tears of joy for the ascension to the next phase.

Aal slithered onto Mary's shoulder, wiped away a tear.

"Indeed, it was a memorable graduation to match a remarkable transformation," he said.

The two stared into the water for a second.

"I am sorry to remind you that in the morning I am leaving for my voyage."

"Yes, of course I remember. I will miss you," Mary said.

"I will miss you too, Mary."

"We will be here waiting for your postcards to arrive." She smiled.

Aal still appreciated the art of hand-written correspondence, and his postcards and letters could be counted on whenever he was away even though his speed of travel meant that from more exotic destinations, the mail he sent while there arrived long after he returned.

"I will also send you anything I hear back from the council in Edinburgh regarding the rogue Soul Reaper."

Mary and Aal were soon interrupted as a few of the guests began departing. She stood up to say her goodbyes to each of the guests, who had traveled from all over the European continent for the memorable ceremony.

15

The day after Gerald's graduation party, most of the Tragically Dead chose to sleep in, recovering from the late-night revelry.

As midday approached, Mary suggested everyone recover with a lazy luncheon in the nearby Vondel Park. Fresh air and leisurely pastimes were just what they needed.

Questions arose about Aal. He hadn't been seen all morning, and if they were going to the park, his club of players were excited to have him referee a "Towers and Portals" tournament. The eel invented the game and usually led its play at what they referred to as "the hex," the garden at Vondel divided into a hexagonal grid.

"Aal has left for his annual Grand Tour," Mary said. "He will return in a few weeks, so for now, someone else will need to manage the tournament."

An impassioned discussion broke out among that portion of the group, deciding who should organize the tournament instead of Aal. Then, what rules should be applied and how the teams should be split up. To those not interested in the game, this was a tiresome affair. Darkhorse returned to his room at the first mention of the game to gather his comic books and make sure his headphones were charged. After a while, others left the room in droves to pack for the excursion.

They gathered various picnic supplies, blankets, baskets, and things to throw, fly or float. Eventually, the entire rambunctious herd bounded down the stairs to the front of the house carrying their chosen toys, equipment and supplies. The congregation of the dead in recovery amassed in the street, excitedly chattering and laughing, with one exception: the doe.

Fawn was understandably not so joyous. Clearly, she didn't have much desire to leave the house for a picnic. Mary imagined what it must have felt like for her, rising that morning with her very best friend gone forever. Mary was reminded of her abandonment of Peter. Fawn must have similar feelings as Peter did when Mary abruptly ended their friendship.

If she left Fawn to sulk at home alone, the doe's malaise would only grow. So, she guided her out the door, promising her a nice surprise.

Mary and the doe were the last to descend the stoop, just as everyone was beginning the journey to the park. Mary announced, "All right everyone, we will meet at the Vondel monument by the pond, but Tycho, Fawn and I will take a scenic route. Go directly there. We will meet you just as you arrive."

"How could we meet them when they arrive if we go a longer way? You are the slowest bicyclist I know," Fawn wondered out loud.

Mary placed the doe into the front basket of her bike, and Tycho perched himself in the center of Mary's handlebars. They backed out of the rows of parked bicycles and joined the procession of dead animals heading south along *Herengracht*. Tycho faced forward and cooed a magical, purr-like melody before extending his wings. Mary sped up, and it looked like she would run into the back of a cluster of her friends.

"What are you doing?" Fawn exclaimed.

Mary said, "Hold on, Fawn, here we go!"

The trio ascended at a steep angle into the air, clearing over the heads of everyone ahead of them, and then veering over in line with the tree-lined canal, while still ascending. Fawn tilted her head over the edge of the cargo basket, peering down at the crowd of her friends. They were cheering and waving as the trio flew over the glistening canal. The bridges and boats shrunk further and further away, and Mary could see their reflection in the water against the sky. Soon, they cut above the rows of canal houses, where it could be seen that many of the gables that crowned the homes were merely facades. Everything was different from the air, compared to the view from the ground. The doe looked back at Mary and the raven in amazement. Tycho's wings flapped leisurely as the sun glistened off his golden bill and wind blew around them. Mary smiled down at the doe and winked.

The bike pitched and bowed along with the air, gliding through the combined control of Mary and Tycho. The doe's glee soon developed into exuberance, and she placed her two front hooves over the edge of the basket and squinted into the wind.

Soon, they approached the immensely lush greenery of the vast park. It was green, so green! The strip of land that made up the park was a large emerald garden contrasting with the red terra-cotta roofs of some more significant buildings that bordered the southern side.

As they flew west over the length of the park, streams and pathways carved out organic shapes throughout the long, rectangular park. Ornamented like a painting, the park appeared daubed with patches of flowers and rows and bunches of bushes and trees, which at this distance looked like mere vegetable stalks.

Mary, Tycho, and Fawn gently weaved a serpentine path high above the park for a few minutes. When they reached the far southwest corner, they banked right and descended into an archway of tree canopy created by two long lines of tall, lush trees on either side of the long flat straightaway at the northern path of the park. Racing through the vast tunnel of foliage, sunlight danced on their faces, flickering. High above the broad dirt path, they cruised over the jittery forms of the living beneath them. The trail veered right, but they went on, ascending through the foliage and then out, continuing east and coasting over the clay tennis courts below to make a direct path to the section where they were to meet the others.

A vast grassy area surrounded the monument to the great Dutch writer Joost van den Vondel, for whom the park was named. They touched down gently onto the soft lawn, and Fawn giggled as Mary propped the bike up on its retractable stand.

The others arrived, led by Darkhorse, and the little doe bounced energetically as they each expressed amazement at what they witnessed. This newfound ability Tycho offered was marvelous and still delighted even him. The doe ran over to the group and relayed the magnificence of viewing the park from the air.

"You guys gotta try it! Everyone, line up!" the little doe insisted, and a good portion of them did. Mary's eyes widened as a long line formed. "One ice-cream token per ride!"

Mary wanted to let the doe have her way today and asked Tycho if he minded, and he agreed to take whoever wanted on a few more trips above the park.

Some of the dead ignored the amusement and passed on, determined to start the giant live-action game Towers and Portals. Eagerly, they headed off to the garden to begin setting up the field.

Over the course of the morning, several groups piled onto Mary and the bike. Stacks of the Tragically Dead, some who borrowed ice-cream tokens for Fawn to collect, lined up patiently and were treated to the spectacle of the scenic park from a new angle, soaring above. Each short trip carried as many as Mary could manage for a few thrilling minutes circling above the park.

In the open grassy meadow, others tossed disks or kicked balls back and forth, but many just enjoyed the outdoors, lazing on blankets, smoking, sipping beverages of their choice or munching on snacks.

After about thirty minutes or so, Tycho and Mary managed to give everyone who wanted a ride. Now she was ready for some relaxation, and Mary reclined on the grass under the shade of a willow tree. The doe curled up next to her and took a nap. Tycho looked like he still had plenty of energy after the sorties. He fluttered alone over the park, diving and darting in and out of the many trees and shady alcoves of Vondel Park.

IN AN ARCHITECTURAL GARDEN section of the park referred to as the hex, a dozen or so of Mary's friends were dressed in costumes carrying enchanted play-weapons. They were warming up for Towers and Portals, scuttling about, passing through portals in the walls of hedges.

But the bulk of the Tragically Dead in Recovery gathered in pockets surrounding the Vondel monument, where Mary was lounging nearby reading under the shade of a tree. The doe had finished counting the ice-cream tokens she'd collected in exchange for rides over the park and lay curled up beside Mary. Darkhorse wore headphones and sat leaning on the trunk of a massive willow tree deep under its shade.

Tycho took the opportunity to test the limits of his enchanted bill, lifting and transporting what appeared to be impossibly massive boulders and then dropping them from great heights into the park's ponds, resulting in extraordinary splashes that impressed and entertained afterlife onlookers.

He flew over to the tree above Mary and perched in a low branch.

"This is a very nice park!"

"I'm glad you like it, Tycho. Just remember to be respectful. Please don't move things around too much. Leave the Picasso in place," Mary implored. He promised he would stay away from all large human-made sculptures from now on.

"What's this game that they are playing in the garden?" asked Tycho.

"Towers and Portals. It's a game Aal invented," Darkhorse

said. He explained that it was a competitive, live-action role-playing game. The experience was augmented with magic. Large playfield elements were designed specifically for integration into the park's unique hexagonal garden. Consisting of a handy grid of six-sided patches of grass and bushes, it was perfect for balancing team territory. In Aal's absence a veteran of the game, a zebra, stepped in to fill the role.

The components of the game were enchanted for convenience. They were pocket-sized and could be stored and carried. With a simple recitation, each game piece or playfield element would grow to full size for installation and play. As the name of the game suggests, there were fortresses with platform towers and tunnels with portals. Each player had developed their unique avatar, and when inhabiting their character, they could choose from various weapons appropriate for their character class. AI knights were used strategically, and depending on how they were set by the team, would attack and defend as convincingly as a living soldier beneath armor. They either defended the tops of towers or guarded entry to a team's portals.

A large billboard calculated scores in real time and displayed across from a modest set of grandstands erected with capacity for about two dozen spectators.

Quite a rivalry had grown between team Hagelslag and team Kapsalon. Word had gotten out that a game was afoot, and a crowd of friends from the outskirts gathered in the hex garden to root on their favorite team.

16

"How is it that Aal became so wise and magical?" Tycho asked Mary.

Mary took a deep breath and replied, "Well, Aal is one of a kind."

"That's for sure," the doe quipped.

"He is also very old, residing in the afterlife longer than anyone I've met here, certainly longer than any of us. But even as a living mortal, Aal possessed extraordinary talents and developed inclinations that grew out of his voracious, curious mind. He had a brazen streak of non-conformity. Eels are not meant to acquire much knowledge, and it is probably the forbidden aspect of his ability to acquire knowledge that spurned him on to continue to expand his intelligence and skills beyond what his original brain was designed for."

"If he is so wise, why doesn't he graduate like Gerald?" the Fawn asked.

"The choice to pass on from the afterlife is a very personal decision. You'd have to ask him." Mary didn't say so, but she believed that Aal liked who he was and was holding onto the fame and identity he had attained. She hadn't thought of it in that way before, and it was something about the way her words sounded to her that made her look at her perspective on her mentor in a new way. She was a little ashamed when she caught herself judging Aal in that moment.

"Is it rude if I ask you how he died?" asked Fawn.

"No, not at all... Aal is not shy about the way he was killed. In fact, his death is well documented, as it is directly connected to a major event in Amsterdam history known as Palingoproer or the Eel Riots of 1886."

"Wow, his death caused a riot?" asked Tycho. "I wonder if anyone cared that I was killed."

"You gotta tell us about this now," said the doe.

Knowing that Aal wouldn't mind, Mary acquiesced and sat up. Her posture drew the attention of the other Tragically Dead. They could always tell when she was about to tell a good story. Even those who already knew the story were eager to hear Mary retell it. A large group gathered around to hear how Aal arrived in the Amsterdam afterlife.

"Aal was born in 1674, during Amsterdam's golden age. He loved to swim through Amsterdam's network of canals and locks. This was not unusual for an eel. What was unusual was that Aal was a long-lived eel with a mutated brain that afforded him all the benefits of human knowledge like speech and logic. The more he learned, the more his mind's ability grew, until his genius rivaled that of even the wisest humans. Over the course of his long life, his mind evolved to tap into a mystical source, and he developed a modest set of benign magical abilities in the living realm. Traveling up and down the waterways of Holland, Aal chose carefully who he revealed himself to. In most cases it was only safe to appear like just another eel of standard intelligence. But throughout his travels across the continent, he acquired multiple languages, and through a series of friendships garnered a legion of influential friends beyond Amsterdam.

"In the nineteenth century, a brutal pastime had developed. It was particularly popular in summer months in the Jordaan district of Amsterdam and was called "eel pulling." Aal, despite his genius and magical abilities, was trapped trying to help a victim of physical abuse. The cruel man who trapped him gave him over for use in the next day's eel pulling, and Aal was suspended alive, secured by a knot around the base of his head, and the rope was strung up across the canal so his body rested a man's height above the canal. With spectators cheering on the competition, Aal was subjected to a sequence of competitors who would pass under while standing on a small, open boat. One after another, men would reach up and attempt to grasp Aal and pull him down with their grip. These inhumane events always drew a raucous and intoxicated crowd.

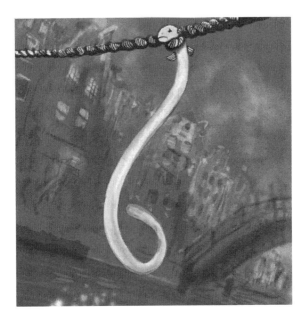

"Soon, police arrived, eager to break up the rowdy assembly, and demanded everyone return home. But they ignored the order and continued the event. The police captain sent officers into the house where one end of the ropes was suspended, to cut it down. When the heavy rope snapped, it twisted and whipped into the portion of the crowd below. A small child who didn't know how to swim fell into the canal, and the crowd furiously erupted. Police at that time had already committed well-documented acts of callousness toward the citizenry of the working-class neighborhood, and this event was simply the tipping point. Aal died after using the last of his magic to save the drowning child, and the crowd filtered into a mob, which rioted into the evening, and again the next day.

"Aal died there in the canal from his injuries as the Eel Riots roared around him, eventually killing almost thirty Amsterdammers. Like all of us, he found a surprisingly welcome charter in the afterlife. Upon arriving in this realm, he spent several years serving each guardian haven in Europe, as well as Tokyo, New York, and San Francisco. He is respected and liked by all rungs of society. Everywhere I go people ask me about Aal. Everyone seems to love that eel. And what is not to love? He has developed into quite the 'gentle-eel.'"

Mary chuckled at her goofy word invention and looked up to find her audience in a somber mood after the harrowing tale of Aal's demise.

She tried to end on a positive note. "You all have minds now that have far more potential than they had when you were alive. You have the capacity now to learn more than you could have when you were alive. The afterlife holds many possibilities for you. That is what Aal and I are so devoted to helping you find."

"Thank you, Mary," Tycho said.

Then a few others joined in and hugged Mary.

"Yes, thank you, Mary," Fawn said, wide-eyed, looking up in a childish, mocking tone. "You know what I think of when I hear a great story like that?"

"What?" said Mary.

"I think of the wise philosopher Pountsemy."

"What?" Mary laughed. "Pountsemy?"

"Okay. Pounce me? You asked for it!" In genuinely affectionate roughhousing, the little doe pounced playfully upon Mary just as she had tricked her into requesting.

Soon Mary was inundated, roaring with laughter under a pile of furry, affectionate Tragically Dead friends.

Darkhorse replaced his headphones and returned to his comic.

NEARLY ALL OF them were gathered together in the area surrounding the Vondel monument preparing to leave at the agreed-upon time. All except for the Towers and Portals players, who seemed to go beyond the agreed-upon timeframe every time. Mary and the others lazed on the lawn, enjoying the fresh spring breeze. The group who'd played football in the meadow were resting under the shade, and Tragically Dead birds continued to play, darting and diving over the water, relishing the warm sun.

They were the first to draw attention to a mysterious bubbling in the pond. Black smoke began covering the surface of the water, then minor splashing began. It drew Mary's immediate attention, and Darkhorse, peeking out from below his hood, moaned with forlorn, "This can't be good."

Mary's fear was realized. The head of the deranged Soul Reaper emerged, its eyes transfixed on Mary. She stood up and shouted, "Everyone, go! Leave the park. Run home as fast as you can. Darkhorse will lead you!"

Darkhorse rolled over. His headphones fell off his head as he rose and attempted to shepherd the Tragically Dead. Some were able to follow, but others stood transfixed by the spectacularly horrifying menace rising from the water.

Frustrated, Mary told them, "Stay away from it. Whatever

happens, avoid its mist if it comes after you! Please go with Darkhorse, now!"

The creature had almost completely emerged. Its dark cloak dripped with silt, pond water, and algae, clinging to its oversized humanoid skeleton. The bubbles that rose around it emitted the dangerous vapor, and around him it grew thick and curled about.

Mary was surrounded by her trembling Tragically Dead friends. They pulled at her dress and hid behind her as she tried in vain to convince them to go home with Darkhorse. Little Fawn ran past Mary and the others, charging without fear straight up under the shadow of the creature.

"Leave us alone, ugly swamp monster!" she shouted, then turned her small body around, rearing up.

It ignored the doe's threat, reaching its arm out toward Mary and letting out its terrifying shriek.

"I said get BACK!" The doe struck with a fierce double-hoof buck to the shin of the beast, and it buckled, lowering its massive skeleton hands to guard against further attacks from the vicious doe.

Fawn reared up and bucked again, this time hitting the beast at the side of its knees with her hard, sharp cloven hooves, and the beast crumbled further. Finally, with a third devastating blow against its posterior, the beast lost its balance and fell, crashing into the water with a deep, guttural yelp.

Aside from Fawn, half of the Tragically Dead heeded her demand and were running home over the canals and through alleyways to get home as quickly as possible. The other half of her innocent friends were either utterly frozen in fear, huddled together in pockets or scampering about, nervously running in a panic. They seemed reluctant to leave the safety of Mary's side. But again, she implored, this time more sternly, "Go home with Darkhorse!"

They finally seemed to listen and moved swiftly toward the

park. Only Mary, Tycho and Fawn remained to face the terrifying Soul Reaper.

The beast recovered and lunged out of the water, slapping the doe and casting her aside. She landed in the shallow water near the shore as Tycho flew overhead and dropped a very large rock but narrowly missed the creature, creating a massive splash that distracted the monster long enough for the raven to swoop down and claw ferociously at the beast's head. The massive Soul Reaper swiped its large heavy skeletal hands at the flapping raven. Tycho pecked violently at the beast, losing a few feathers, and eventually latched onto the thick sopping hood of the beast.

As he began to lift the threatening creature away, it looked up and screamed, emitting a blast of putrid gas that hit the top of its hood but partially curled around and reached the nostrils of the raven. It would have easily killed the raven had the thick core of the blast not been divided and muffled. The lesser exposure to the mist still led Tycho to flutter away in distress. He collapsed on the shore, feathers a mess and his golden beak opened wide, gasping for fresh air.

The beast lunged toward Mary, knocking back the doe with his arm before she could finish her wind-up. The spry Fawn landed on her side but quickly rolled over and hopped onto her feet, then headed over to assist Tycho to safety.

Mary clasped her pendant, tilted her head down and flashed a furious glare at the creature. "You came for me, Soul Reaper. You've harmed my friends, and now you must face my wrath."

Power surged through her body, and the talisman amplified her protective rageful intention. A powerful blast of energy shot out from her forehead and struck the beast in the center of its chest, knocking it high in the air, clear across the pond.

The monster landed hard, pressing deep into the swampy wetland, facedown. It lay there motionless.

"Daaaaaamn!" the doe exclaimed standing on the shore.

Initially relieved, Mary quickly felt a pang of guilt. If this ended the creature, it was the first time she had ever done such a thing. Trying to get a better look, she stepped toward the water. She looked back to see if Tycho had recovered enough to fly her over there. He was still upon the back of the doe, stretching his wings and coughing. She was relieved to see her friends in better shape than she'd feared.

"Mary, look!" said Fawn.

From across the water, the Soul Reaper crawled up and hobbled off, to disappear into the wooded area to the west. Mary looked back to make sure Darkhorse and her friends were well gone. They were out of sight, hopefully headed east toward home.

Tycho fluttered over to Mary. "I think he is headed in the direction of the hex garden. The Towers and Portals players are still there, remember?"

"Yes, are you all right?"

"I'm fine. Let's take your bike!" Tycho said and brought it over.

Mary placed Fawn in the front basket, and together on her bicycle they soared over the pond toward the trees.

17

M ary, Tycho, and Fawn approached the players from the air and landed right on the holographic central tower, interrupting the game. Unaware of the emergency, the referee zebra incredulously called a time-out.

"We are almost done, Mary!"

"Sorry, Zeke, there is a serious menace attacking us here in the park. It is not safe. Darkhorse has led an evacuation of the others. I need you to get everyone here back to the house at once."

The severity of Mary's concern, conveyed the seriousness of the situation. Zeke turned pale and immediately called off the game. Spectators in the stands booed, but Fawn approached and explained the situation, suggesting they also head back to their homes with caution. In mere seconds, the massive game elements and grandstands were shrunk down and placed in a box and a satchel with a drawstring, and they quickly headed home with the same level of alertness they'd been practicing in the game.

Mary and Tycho flew swiftly west in pursuit of the beast. They searched diligently, weaving in and out of the park, and beyond. They kicked up dust around pathways, slid over the surface of dark waters, and combed under wooded areas, in attempts to locate the monster—to no avail.

BACK AT THE HOUSE, Darkhorse led the last of the now terrified dead in recovery up the stairs. The slow-moving tortoise was the last member of the group he led in. Just as he was about to close the front door, Darkhorse paused to glance up and down the canal to be certain there were no stragglers. He heard a splash in the canal. He was shocked when he looked over the bikes parked along the edge of the canal. Fearing the worst, he paused, squinting to see if it could be the beast, but it stopped and he secured the door.

Upstairs, the Tragically Dead speculated on what the Soul Reaper was after. As Darkhorse locked the door, he heard a bird joke, "Maybe it was trying to recruit Darkhorse." The cynical birds chuckled nervously. Darkhorse understood the reference to his skeletal remains and black cloak, but he was numb to their insensitive barb. Darkhorse was concerned with keeping everyone safe, as Mary would want. Everyone was a bit on edge after what they saw in the park, and if making him the target of jokes helped relieve their tension, he could handle it. He headed up the stairs.

In the main room, Darkhorse did his best to manage the situation and lowered his voice to address the vulnerable group.

"Everybody, quiet down. This is serious. We don't know what this thing is or what it wants. Mary will stop it if she can, but we must be as quiet and cautious as possible. The safest place is up in Mary's attic suite in the rear annex. It will be tight, but we can all fit there. I suggest we go there, but we must do so quietly. I doubt this thing will come for us, but let's not take any chances, eh?" They all nodded in agreement. "I will secure all the doors as we go."

The group ascended the stairs as quietly as they could. The tortoise would take almost an hour to climb the stairs on his own, so to get him up from the floors below, a legion of mice got under the tortoise, and together they scurried, carrying him up to the main room on the next series of floors like a reverse mudslide of black and brown fur. In their nervousness, a few others of the Tragically Dead tripped over steps, making rather loud fury thumps, followed by nearly as loud sighs, shushes and reprimands.

None, though, made as much noise as Dom, the fox. Fearing for his rare coin collection, and against better judgement, he balanced three glass jars of coins in his thin arms as he climbed the stairs. Behind him followed a mole who was eager to get up the stairs and ascended too quickly, his sensitive nose tickled by the slowly ascending fox's tail, and he sneezed and bumped into the fox, which led him to drop the top jar. It shattered, and the sound of hundreds of VOC coins loudly rang, pinged and echoed as they cascaded down the wooden stairway. Dom was embarrassed, and also wanted desperately to gather them up, but was instead rushed up the stairs by the incensed Darkhorse, who whisper-shouted, "We'll get them later!"

As they settled into Mary's room, Darkhorse locked the door. Fearful speculation about the Soul Reaper was being whispered but was interrupted when they heard a loud bang on the front door. They discussed it quietly, and several established that it wasn't a knock like a salesman or a nosy neighbor, it was much more malevolent in nature, like the butt of a heavy assault rifle.

A rabbit suggested, "Well it might just be the gestapo, like during the occupation."

"How would that be any better?" asked one of the mice.

The next hit was more violent, and a real sense of terror struck as the front door sounded as if it were completely smashed in. Nothing was heard for a few moments after that.

"Maybe she forgot her key," said Walter, the tiniest brown mouse, who was being held in the wings of one of the bats.

"Mary wouldn't tear the door open, idiot," said one of the birds.

The entire group held onto one another, the tiniest embraced the small, the small clung to the medium, and the largest held them all. None of them had experienced this level of terror in their entire afterlives, and most not even in their tragically ended lives.

A few moments of anxious silence gave false hope that there was nothing to worry about. But then the sound of heavy footsteps echoed up the stairs toward the chamber door.

Darkhorse struggled to make peace with his impending fate. On one hand he was angry that he hadn't made more progress in the afterlife, but in some ways, he was prepared to either move on or be sent back to the living realm. Just two days before, he cursed the fact that he couldn't drown, he could only suffer. He doubted that he would advance to join Gerald and other graduated friends in the beautiful maelstrom of subconscious leading to the next stage of existence.

A *bang!* at the chamber door startled all of them. Darkhorse stood protectively at the front of the group, front hooves spread wide in a futile effort to guard his friends. When the door burst open, Darkhorse shouted out to the darkness, "No! Get out of here! This is our safe haven!"

He heard soft thuds behind him. He looked down to see several of the Tragically Dead had fainted. The Soul Reaper was obscured by his smoky aura, which began to creep menacingly into the room.

It was curling and swirling as if it was hunting for a victim, feeling out the width of the room. Slowly, the hooded beast emerged from the mist, its eyes hollow, and its teeth clenched as it surveyed the group, sweeping slowly left then right, then up over them as if it too was searching for something – apparently, not them.

One of the players from team Hagelslag reached into his satchel and threw out a Mage Knight figurine. The beast looked down at the small game figurine, barely the size of the smallest mouse. The player shouted "Game on!" and the piece grew to the size of a tall human, glowing and animated, holding up a large majestic sword.

It convincingly asserted, "You who have climbed the tower of Hagelslag, return to your origin or face my deadly blade!"

The beast cocked its head like a curious dog. As it did, the tortoise who was standing just by the doorway, under Mary's coatrack, took the opportunity to attempt to escape – very slowly of course.

The holographic knight swung a massive sword in the direction of the beast. Startled, the Soul Reaper stepped backward through the doorway, tripped over the slowly exiting tortoise, and fell down the stairs like a heavy sack of large bones. The group's terror turned to curiosity when the monster tumbled down all five stairways.

"That'll teach it," said Walter, the little brown mouse.

"Quick, barricade the door," said Darkhorse.

Each of the Tragically Dead picked up as much furniture, books and other items as they could. Mary's attic suite was a good size, containing her counselor's parlor, desk area and library, and bedroom. In the desperation of the moment, they quickly stacked items haphazardly against the suite's door.

A few of the Tragically Dead threw a rope around the hook of the gable and were queuing up to climb down when the beast's thick, sooty mist seeped through the pile at the door. Ten or so had already made it out the window and were descending a hoisting rope desperate to escape.

"There's Mary!" called out a polecat as he reached for the rope.

Mary, Fawn and Tycho appeared, swooping over the top of the tree, and entered through one of the tall open windows past the rope and into the suite.

MARY LEAPT from the bike before it touched on the floor and charged past the crowd of Tragically Dead toward the chamber door, shouting, "Everyone move to the front, near the windows. Open them all, make sure you don't breathe the black mist from the monster."

With her pendant in hand, she blasted the pile aside to confront the Soul Reaper, and Fawn bounced on Mary's bed with anticipation. "Let him have it!"

Mary flung open the door and shouted the into the dark, soot-filled stairwell, "The afterlife is our domain. You have no authority here, Soul Reaper!"

Aside from thin vapor, it was empty. The monster was not there.

"He's getting away!" a shout from the window called out.

Mary ran over and leaned out the window. The beast hobbled away along the canal.

"Does this mean we should go back inside now?" asked a boar, grunting as he was losing his grip.

A handful of Tragically Dead greeted her there, struggling as they hung onto the rope from the hook.

Mary summoned Tycho to quickly ferry her down to the ground. "Now get them down safely and come find me."

Mary raced away in pursuit of the beast, her toes hovering just off the ground and a blue swirl encompassing her. Her determination pushed her faster than she'd ever gone while hovering, and her pendant glowed brightly.

The creature paused at an alleyway entrance and glanced back at Mary, then continued, hastily limping into the alley as if alarmed at her pursuit. Mary sped ahead, turned down the alley, and found it at the other end. Just before she reached it, the Soul Reaper surprised Mary when he hopped on the jittery shadow form of a living-realm vehicle – a motor scooter – and sped quickly away. She followed the trail of black mist, passing without hesitation through the souls of the living and the dead.

She caught up to the scooter, but before she reached it, the monster leapt off, transferring to the hazy shadow of a living-realm delivery truck. Mary chased the vehicle over the shadows of tram lines on *Spuistraat*. When the truck stopped behind other vehicles at a traffic light, the beast ditched it, hobbling desperately on foot among other stopped living vehicles to get away from her.

A black sedan came speeding past, its right tires on the sidewalk and its left in the gutter. The Reaper jumped on. The car turned off the ledge, flat onto the cobblestone street, and accelerated, racing past the palace along the edge of Dam Square. Mary cut through the square, catching up to it as it roared past the tall war memorial monument and stopped at a hotel on the edge of the red-light district.

The beast leapt off it and scurried into the crowded pedestrian traffic. Living tourists experienced gusts of cold wind as both the creature and Mary passed quickly through their bodies. She chased it through de Wallen and into one of the alleys lined with glowing red windows, inhabited by the silhouettes of living forms peering out at the ruckus.

Mary felt compassion for every soul around her, except for the monster.

18

Under the ruby light of the narrow passage, she clasped her talisman and conjured two energy barriers. One placed beyond the creature and the other behind Mary. The beast struck the force field. It looked up desperate to escape the alley, so Mary manifested another barrier above. There was no eluding her now. The monster fell to its knees.

Every attempt to treat it with kindness only led to aggression, and the attacks on her innocent friends left Mary no choice. She took her pendant in hand and reached deep into her soul. It was time to end this. Her eyes glowed silvery white. Her black lips parted to reveal menacing elongated cuspids. Bursting free from her usual up-do, Mary's hair swirled, defying gravity like the dynamic crown of a dark queen of the afterlife. A maelstrom powered by love, light, and magic churned around her. This threat now awakened her inner warrior.

"Time for mercy has long passed," she told the Soul Reaper.

The monster arose. It towered over Mary facing off in the alleyway. As it leaned its head back, the creature unhinged its jaw and ejected another piercing shriek with bundle of toxic vapor hurtling straight toward her face. Mary kept still, grinning menacingly as the grim plume parted around her head. An invisible wedge divided and rerouted it past the sides of her as she stood defiantly. It was her turn to respond.

Mary's eyes glowed blue, then an entirely radiant white. She exuded a blast of power from her forehead. For a split second, the Soul Reaper appeared to recede back before the loud crack of energy landed. The blinding flash of light threw the monster forcefully across the alley, slamming it into a thick section of the stone wall. The Reaper's black cloak and mist lay lifeless, and the fumes dissipated. Dust and chips of graffiti paint rained onto the beast where he fell.

She hovered over to finish it, proclaiming, "I am Mary van Amsterdam, you who dare to trespass in my territory have no power here. Our love rejects your very nature!"

Bright beams of light emitted from the talisman in all directions. Between her eyes, a spot on the center of her forehead glowed. She screamed in fury as the energy from an innate spell built and passed through her. The rows of red lamplight in the alley flickered. The floor-to-ceiling windowed doors bowed and vibrated violently like enormous soap bubbles. Souls from both realms closed curtains, retreating to safety. The words Mary yelled next were neither English, nor Dutch, nor any living realm language.

Mary screamed, and a fierce whirlwind of energy swelled around her. She leaned back, then directed a burst straight at the beast, paired with a spherical shockwave. The windows exploded. The ground beneath them cracked and shifted in an instant. The Soul Reaper's face held terror in the millisecond before the blast of sand and vapor obscured Mary's view of its annihilation.

The maelstrom settled. As it did, it revealed that what now lay before Mary was only a pile of pulverized stone, clumps of red brick, and dust. The dark affectations of her rage diminished, and she returned to normal. Had Mary vanquished it? She combed through the rubble, but found no sign of the Soul Reaper. Buildings on either side of the alley, jolted by the blast, creaked and swayed as if breathing again. Witnesses, from both the dead and the living realms, took notice.

Overwhelmed and relieved, Mary fell to her knees.

Now things could get back to normal. She stood slowly and turned around. Through dark locks of hair draped down her face she saw a group of Tragically Dead friends surrounded by strangers. A crowd had gathered in the alley, their mouths all agape. Darkhorse's cracked jaw had never been so open. Even mouthy Fawn was initially dumbstruck.

The mass of gawkers grew dense as both dead and living residents clamored around the scene. Muffled sounds of sirens whined and the far-off sound of a living realm police helicopter batted overhead through the membrane separating life from the hereafter. Obviously the event made a significant cross-dimensional impact.

Mary stepped through the crowd, gathered her friends, and departed. As she did, she ignored comments and questions from the afterlife residents.

"What was that?" a woman asked.

"It was a Soul Reaper," someone said.

"Did that Soul Reaper come for you, Mary?"

"Are you allowed to kill a Soul Reaper?"

"Is that Mary van Amsterdam?"

"What happened?"

"Who did she banish?"

Instantly murmurs became rumors, and rumors became lies. Confusion about the dramatic details of the incident swept through the crowd. Mary didn't have the energy to explain her actions. This was a personal battle, and her role as guardian of the Amsterdam Afterlife gave her free rein to carry out her obligations any way she saw fit.

After ensuring her friends were unharmed, Mary gathered her hair once again into a high bun. She took a front hoof of Darkhorse into her hand, and said in a daze, "Let's go home now, shall we?"

MARY AND DARKHORSE walked together behind the doe who had no qualms parting the crowd to lead the small group of Tragically Dead home.

The Amsterdam night grew chilly. Without outer wear, Mary held her bare arms in her hands. Darkhorse offered his cloak, but she kindly refused. Eyes drawn downward, a morsel of shame in her stomach soon turned to nausea as she walked. Her blind destructive wrath had taken her by surprise, emerging so quickly and from deep within her. A part of her wondered if she'd done the right thing. Mary had never even considered harming another being, let alone utterly vanquishing them into oblivion.

If justified, she still worried about the potential misperception of the confrontation. Witnesses to the final encounter in the alley would be correct in saying the Soul Reaper was the one running from Mary. She was the "perpetrator" seen pursuing and attacking the "victim." Would she have to defend her actions in the court of public opinion? Aal and the council would protect her. Or would they? Worry and uncertainty now overcame Mary.

In contrast to Mary's morose mood, Fawn was exuberant as she strutted in front of the group. She strolled along as if on a fashion runway, head held high.

"Did you guys see that?" she shouted at a passerby, "It put the damn in Mary van Amsterdam!"

Mary looked over to Darkhorse.

He said, "If I had eyes, you'd see them rolling."

Mary chuckled, grateful for a brief relief from her worry.

Not everyone in the Amsterdam Afterlife was aware of what happened in the alley yet, so Fawn took it upon herself to change that.

"Did you feel that massive explosion from the red-light district? That was her." She pointed with her nose. "My friend Mary van Amsterdam. She just destroyed a Soul Reaper!"

A stranger ignored Fawn, only glancing at Mary before evading eye-contact. Dismissing the shy, dead Dutchman, the doe scurried across the cobblestone to appeal to a different audience. A small group of men and women sat smoking and drinking on a stoop as she approached.

With her front hoof, she pointed and said, "That is Mary van Amsterdam, the guardian of the Tragically Dead in Recovery, and she just totally annihilated a Soul Reaper!"

The group cheered, half-interested, and raised glasses celebrating the doe's odd enthusiasm. Mary would have objected if she wasn't so lost in her own thoughts.

After cutting through the *Romeinsarmsteeg* alleyway, they reached the canal house. While the doe continued to reveal out front, Mary climbed the stairs and entered the large main room where the Tragically Dead had assembled.

"What happened?" Dom, the fox asked.

"The birds reported a huge blast from the east side. Is everything okay?" asked Bas, the littlest mouse.

"I will fill you all in on the details. Let's make sure we're all safe and accounted for. Everyone, locate your safety partner."

Eager to hear the news, the Tragically Dead shuffled around and found their partner assigned in the event an emergency or on excursions to large public spaces.

"Great, looks like we have everybody." Before Mary could continue, Fawn burst past her to the center of the room.

"You guys should have seen it! Mary got all wicked, with glowy eyes." The doe's eyes crossed. "She unleashed all hell on that thing!"

"I am not wicked," Mary corrected with a shy, somewhat flustered smile.

"Wait, you're wicked now?" a bat said delighted by the notion.

"No, I am not wicked now."

"I didn't say you are wicked, I said you got wicked. It's a good thing, you saved us. You probably even saved all of Amsterdam. That thing was crazy scary and creepy. It got what it deserved for attacking us!"

"Fawn, please, stop interrupting!" Mary demanded.

"You did totally annihilate it though," the doe murmured with her head down but her eyes up.

"So is this true? Did you banish it?" a bird asked.

"I believe so. We are safe again. As your guardian, I shall always do my best to keep you safe. That is why I am here.

Since I have dispatched the Soul Reaper, we must return to our regular routines again. I'll schedule sessions all day tomorrow to catch us up. Now, get some rest. Your progress matters most. Everything will return to normal in the morning."

They begged Mary to tell them all she could about the final encounter. She patiently detailed the event and answered an exhausting host of questions.

Mary yearned to retreat to the sanctuary of her attic apartment. "I think you would all agree that it has been a long day," she said finally, maintaining a reassuring smile. "I know I have had quite an evening. I will retire to my suite now to clean up the mess the beast has left behind. Good night, my friends."

19

She saw that Darkhorse was already in her attic suite, in a futile effort to be helpful by sorting through the messy piles of books and furniture.

"Sorry, Mary, I'm not of much use with these clumsy hooves."

"Not to worry, my friend, I can take care of this."

Mary grasped for her pendant and reached out her hand to lift the turned-over vanity furniture but felt no pulse and no glow came from the talisman. She tried again, but once more, nothing. She examined it, turning it over and examining both the front side with its symbols, as well as plain back side, but could find nothing physically wrong with it.

"Is there something wrong with it?" asked Darkhorse.

"I don't know. It's as if it has no energy." Mary finally gave up and threw the silver talisman against the wall. She stood among a constellation of her afterlife possessions, some over-turned, some broken and scattered about, feeling utterly miserable. Her hands fell to her sides and she collapsed on her bed. "I can't believe that this is all happening while Aal is gone. I should have asked him to stay a little longer."

"Mary, I am sorry." Darkhorse knelt beside her bed and placed his hoof on her shoulder. "Mary, we can fix this. At least we don't have to worry about that monster thing anymore."

Mary felt perhaps she was overreacting. She needed to keep it together, otherwise what was this all for?

"That's right, Darkhorse. We'll figure this out. I am so grateful to have you here, my friend. You truly performed admirably today. Thank you."

"I don't know, if I were better, the others would respect me more, and I could have gotten everyone out of the park faster. I didn't notice the beast was following us home. You entrusted me to get everyone home safely, and I failed."

"No, Darkhorse, you didn't fail at all, darling. You were brave. You did a wonderful job and everything worked out for the best. We are all safe, and the Soul Reaper is now gone."

"What are you going to do about your talisman?"

"Well, I suppose I will have to travel to Edinburgh, where it was charmed, and have it looked at. I am not sure what happened, if I overloaded it, or if I have been banished from using it. But I have certainly never felt a magnitude of emotion like that while casting a spell before."

"So, you will take the train tomorrow without Aal?"

"I guess so," she said with a sudden anxious feeling of trepidation. She had a mild fear that perhaps she'd gone too far and the council disenchanted her pendant. What if she was deemed unfit to be guardian of her beloved friends?

Darkhorse interrupted her fearful thoughts, and she realized she was showing worry on her face.

"I would be honored to stay here and watch over the house while you are gone."

"Oh Darkhorse, you will always be my dearest, dead horse friend."

"Mary, that means more to me than you could ever know."

Mary held Darkhorse's right hoof in her hand and nestled her face against the dry bone of his enormous skull.

"Mary, you shouldn't feel guilty about killing that Reaper. He would have killed us all eventually."

Mary paused. A mild urge of compassion to defend the nature of all entities rose within her, but then she was forced to admit to herself that she truly did what she had to do to protect her friends.

They sat quietly for a few moments, then Darkhorse said, "Mary, forgive yourself and move on. Don't let any event hold you back from being the sweet, awesome and amazing person that you are."

In his efforts to reassure Mary, Darkhorse had revealed that he was growing wiser. His profound words seemed to echo. He momentarily stared off as if he was internalizing his own advice. He sat up. Mary knew just what had happened.

"Mary, this is what I need to do," he said.

"Yes."

"You have been trying to get me to do this all along," he said, astonished.

Mary held her hands, palms together before her lips, smiling. The Tragically Dead fire horse had finally had a breakthrough, an epiphany that she hoped would change the course of his recovery forever. Mary smiled, and rather than obsess over the events with the Reaper, she gladly talked about what Darkhorse needed to do next in his steps to recovery.

After the illuminating discussion wrapped up, Darkhorse excused himself excitedly. Something was very different. Mary closed her door a bit, but not all the way. She was compelled to clean up a bit before bed but then felt a sudden onset of fatigue from the long and active day. Despite her eagerness for sleep, she proceeded to pick up a few of the books off a pile on the ground and place them back on the shelf by hand. Perhaps this would have to wait for tomorrow. Then with a knock of his hoof, Darkhorse reentered with a cavalry of reinforcements. The Tragically Dead spread out across the suite, led by Darkhorse and Fawn. In a few minutes, they had her room back in order. A few things were broken, and a few things were missing. But her room no longer looked like a trash heap, and she could sleep and would catch the train first thing in the morning to face whatever awaited her from the council in Edinburgh.

THE NEXT MORNING, Mary and Tycho awoke and prepared to leave for Edinburgh – but one crucial thing was missing. Her go-bag was gone. She recruited the whole house to search for it inside and out, but it could not be found. What it most crucially held at this time was her Guardian ID, which enabled her train passage. In a rush to get to Edinburgh, she decided to simply have Tycho take her there. She'd simply bundle up in extra layers for the cold voyage. She instinctively grasped her charmed pendant to get dressed, but of course it didn't react.

"Right," she said with a huff, and proceeded to get dressed in the manner of the living.

As she slipped on her thickest hose in anticipation of a chilly voyage without magic over the North Sea, she heard Darkhorse's large bones clattering through the hall and down the stairs. The door opened with only one turn of the lock – uncharacteristic for him. Curious, Mary stopped with only one stocking on and hobbled over to the front window. Was that really him? Darkhorse had no visible bindings at all. His grim horse skeleton galloped full bore, unhindered. She smiled, happy for her friend, and guessed he was headed toward the Key House to share the good news with Jaap.

Just then a legion of messenger orbs lined up and entered her room. Mary sped through the messages as she dressed. Some were indications of support, which worried Mary. What kind of trouble was she in? Some were sharp admonishments or grand praise from complete strangers regarding her now notorious encounter with the rogue Soul Reaper in the red-light district. The afterlife citizenry had heard from alleged witnesses, some who expressed exaggerated or completely inaccurate accounts of the event. All of the sensationalized attention and speculation were adding enough grist for the rumor mill of the afterlife to make Mary van Amsterdam more famous than she already was, but for all the wrong reasons. She didn't want to build notoriety as a warrior. She was a healer and a guardian.

Fawn came bursting into the house with print copies of

every afterlife tabloid. They all had featured the event on the front page. Headlines included "Mad Mary's Meltdown!", "Mary, Mary, Quite Combustible!", "Healer or Reaper Killer?"

To most in the afterlife, the news was puzzling. How could such a benevolent soul justify dispatching an entity as powerful and sovereign as a Soul Reaper? Mary needed Aal's public relations skills, but he was gone, and Mary had no way to reach him.

After receiving ten or so of them, Mary stopped accepting the messenger orbs. She just wanted to get to Edinburgh and find out what was wrong with her pendant. If she had to, she wanted to face the consequences and move on.

Tycho could pull Mary and her bicycle into the air, but without her pendant talisman's powers, she couldn't pass through the ceiling to take off from the attic. So, Mary dragged the bike down the attic stairs to the next floor where the bike could pass through large windows. The steep and narrow stairs made for an awkward transport for Mary. It was unwieldy, and the bicycle tires left several scuff marks on the white walls by the time they reached the bottom. The ordeal made her realize how reliant on her powers she'd become.

At the next floor, Tycho saw her struggling and offered to pull the bicycle through the large windows.

"Oh right, what was I thinking?" Mary said. She hadn't slept well.

Mary descended the interior stairs to the landing and out onto the stoop. Tycho safely delivered her bike to the ground and together they took their positions at the edge of the canal. Mary took her seat and Tycho perched his scaly feet on the center of the cool steel handlebars. With one push on the right pedal, Mary rolled them forward, appearing to afterlife onlookers as if they'd might descend into the water, but instead rose into the wind, gliding over the canal and above the familiar quaint stone bridges of the canal district. They went up and over the rows of houses along the water, soaring past the familiar *Westerkerk* tower and continuing westward out of the city toward the coast. They passed Wijk Aan Zee and its sandy bars and little beach houses crammed together along the coast before crossing high above the North Sea.

"Look how tiny the shadow forms of living windsurfers look below," Mary said.

"They look like they are having fun. Do the Tragically Dead in Recovery ever go to the beach, Mary?"

"We do, but we haven't in a long time. We will go this summer."

"I look forward to that," he said excitedly.

The ride was indeed chilly, and without her talisman charged, Mary was unable to use any special powers to magically stay warm and simply relied on her Amsterdammer gear to keep her warm. Her woolen coat, thick cowl, gloves and leggings could protect her from the nip on the ground, but high in the air, it was barely tolerable.

Mary began to wonder what the council, also known as the Council of Standing Ancients, would have to say. Surely, they'd understand that she was simply fulfilling her role and defending the dead in recovery. But on the other hand, she did destroy a Soul Reaper. Unquestioning obedience was never something that came naturally to Mary. Even from her time in the living realm she was no stranger to obstinance, especially when it came to injustice. It was who she was, and she remembered what Aal had told her: she was chosen for this role because of who she fundamentally was, and if she stayed true to herself, she would excel. If that was true, then no one in the afterlife could rightly condemn her. Her role in the afterlife was to protect her friends, and that was exactly what she did when she dispatched the monster in the alley.

Soon, they saw the coast of Britain. Via the Norfolk coast they turned north to fly along it. They sped past Scarborough and Newcastle Upon Tyne, before turning west along the Northumberland coast. Dunbar made way for their final approach to Edinburgh via the large Firth of Forth. Mary couldn't be more pleased to see the massive extinct volcano known as Arthur's Seat coming up on the horizon, indicating they were approaching their destination. Flying over, they saw on the hill beyond a metropolis of stone and wood neighborhoods leading up to Edinburgh Castle.

Mary landed along the royal mile to what was known as the John Knox House.

"Wow, Mary, I have never seen a place like this," Tycho said as they landed.

It was a very old house with a core built out of stone and whimsical additions attached. Some of the timber galleries hung out over the road. On the ground, spirits of living tourists paraded up and down the mile. Mary and Tycho passed through a mass of them to get near the house.

Aal had once told Mary that it was a very old mansion, in fact the oldest medieval mansion in Edinburgh, built in 1490 and expanded over the centuries. It was marvelous, and Mary took a deep breath, ready to face the council.

As she approached the door, it opened and an old long-dead Scotsman kindly greeted and led her in.

"Welcome, Mary van Amsterdam," he said.

Mary faithfully followed the man. They moved through the dark house and into a large room with ornately carved walls and ceiling. As Mary stood gazing up, the doors swung closed and locked with a loud thump. Mary was left alone in the dark room without the use of her night vision abilities. This would be her second ever meeting with the council. The utter absence of any sounds or sights triggered a moment of deep introspection. It felt like lifetimes ago since she was assigned the role of guardian in the afterlife. She had no idea what awaited her now. Punishment or praise seemed equally likely.

20

After several seconds, Mary detected a faint swirl of green light emitting from the carved shapes above her. It grew brighter and brighter, and she could see every detail of the room's ornamentation. She was softly lifted off the floor and pulled toward the ceiling swirling with green light and tendrils of light mist. She passed through the ceiling into a dark expanse and was tenderly placed onto a soft grassy meadow, and the light faded away.

Her eyes adjusted and she could see stars in the sky as bright as they could be. She was admiring the clarity of the constellations when she realized that there were dark silhouettes of tall stones surrounding her.

The grass gently rustled. She turned and saw an elegant pale woman with a bright red shock of hair, riding a most graceful and marvelous mare. As they neared, Mary realized it wasn't just a mare. From the center of its forehead a long spiraling horn gushed forth. She had never imagined such a picturesque unicorn. It approached and turned its head to deliver warm regards from kind, accepting eyes that gave her a deep sense of benevolent reassurance. The woman atop it was equally breathtaking. She elegantly dismounted and smiled warmly as she stepped up to Mary.

She reached out and held her hand softly and told Mary slowly and with intensity, "Mary, I am Isobel. You have proved yourself to be a worthy and noble guardian." As the woman embraced Mary, a warm comforting energy washed over her and eased all her fears.

Mary was quite certain that she had never met Isobel before, but felt a strong connection to her. Without words, she understood the nonverbal message. She was chosen for good reason. She had faced a new challenge. She had been tested and succeeded. Mary would need even more compassion and confidence to face what would come next.

Mary opened her eyes and noticed jagged, sharp stones illuminated in the darkness in several concentric circles surrounding her. The henge was ancient and weathered, and she sensed an even greater, more ancient power from it than from the angelic Isobel. The massive stones illuminated further, and upon their surface the images of gray aged humans appeared. This was the Council of Standing Ancients.

"Mary van Amsterdam," a deep male voice said, his voice reverberating.

She turned her attention to it and saw the image of a cloaked figure with a long white beard projected onto the rock shape, and when she looked to him, he smiled.

"You have proven yourself to be a well-attuned guardian, more than capable of caring for the Tragically Dead in Recovery. You shall be entrusted with greater power, for soon you will be forced to take on greater responsibilities in the afterlife."

"I am glad that I have done well. All I have ever wanted to do was have the opportunity to fulfill my ideals and ease the suffering of the innocent."

"You have done admirably," one of the other stones said. "Now the council will bequeath greater powers to fulfill your evolving spirit."

At this, Isobel turned and faced Mary, then gently grasped the dead pendant that hung from Mary's neck. One palm took the smooth, unmarked back and the other rested over the side with symbols.

The stone elder spoke again as light leaked out from between Isobel's palms enclosed around the talisman. "You now have two roles, Mary van Amsterdam, guardian and healer of the Tragically Dead in Recovery," he said as Isobel revealed the same shiny silver side of the talisman pendant Mary knew well, but with more symbols.

She then rotated her cupped hands and opened her palm to reveal the other side.

Isobel then spoke. "You now have an equally noble alter-ego: Marij van de Doden, Avenger of the Damned and Mistreated." She lifted her palm to reveal the other side of the pendant. It was shiny black with more symbols of a similar nature to those on the silver side.

With one hand still holding the talisman, Isobel stood and held her other hand to the sky, and from the tops of the ancient standing stones, ethereal fiery crowns appeared. From these crowns, beams of light converged to the raised fist in the center like a lightning rod. Energy and light surged through her into the pendant, and an immense glow engulfed Mary too as she stood beside her.

Mary was struck by images of her past and glimpses into her future. For merely a moment, a rush of details from her living past, some familiar, some forgotten, were vividly relived again. She was confronted with many elements of her past that she had been allowed to forget. The tragedy and trauma of her life were no longer hidden from her. She had a new perspective and distance from herself that allowed her to clearly restore her identity. She remembered clearly her mama and papa, her sister, and her sweetly tragic Peter. She understood the true motives and machinations of the living and some dead that she couldn't before. There remained pockets of blankness, blind spots that she couldn't see, but much more was now known to Mary in that instant than in the past seventy-plus years in the afterlife.

When Mary approached the edge of emotional overload, she collapsed, sobbing into Isobel's gentle embrace, and blacked out. Mary awoke lying on the grass as the woman stroked her cheeks. Mary noticed the faces of the ancients had faded away and stood again as blank stone. Isobel bent down and kissed Mary's forehead, gently laid her down in the meadow, backed away and rode off on her beautiful unicorn mare. Mary lay there in the grass, looking up at the stars in amazement and with the most overwhelming sense of peace and understanding than she had ever had. She closed her eyes, pinching out tears of gratitude.

The door unlatched, and Mary opened her eyes. The man opened the massive, creaking doors, letting in enough light to see naturally without being overwhelmed by the brightness. He led her over to a built-in seat.

"Wait right here."

He left the room for a quick moment and returned with two glasses of Scotch whisky.

"A quick nip should help ya simmer," he said.

"Thank you," she said and took a long sip.

HIGH IN AMSTERDAM'S WESTERTOREN, the bells rang out as they did every fifteen minutes. Arriving at Westerkerk that morning was Beandrus, a beaver assigned as caretaker to the church's bell tower in the afterlife. As he approached the steps to the building, he encountered the saddest lost creature he had ever come across, collapsed on the stairs. It appeared a frightful mouse carcass. "How long have you been lying here?" he wondered to himself. The filthy matted fur and grime indicated perhaps that it had survived a swim in one of the canals, and perhaps had been run over a few times by vehicles. Beandrus couldn't be sure about that but was certain that the creature was just about as near death as anything could be in the dead realm, and that's saying a lot.

"What have you been through, my little friend?" he wondered as he picked up the small mouse into a small white handkerchief. The mouse's tail was bloodied and had coagulated to form a sticky adhesion to the stair and left behind a ring around the malformed body of the tiny rodent.

There was only one place for a spirit in such a state, so the beaver left the church and marched down to *Herengracht* to deliver the suffering spirit to Mary van Amsterdam.

∾

BACK AT THE HOUSE, Darkhorse stood above the group of dead peering at the spectacle. The dead in recovery were crammed, pressed against the glass on the second floor of the house, observing a vibrant parade of floats passing along the canal below. Utilizing the half of the windows on the second floor made of spirit-glass, they could see clearly into the living realm. An endless line of colorful, lively boats packed into the canal for the celebration, adorned with rainbows and dancing humans. Both sides of the canal were crammed with vibrant living observers, and they bounced to a deep dance beat loud enough to cross all the way into the dead realm.

The door rang, and Darkhorse descended the stairs.

He opened the door to find standing before him a somber beaver, cloaked in a tan cowl reminiscent of a little friar.

"Oh hello, Darkhorse, is Mary or Aal available?" the beaver asked.

Darkhorse was taken aback that this beaver he had never met knew his name, and took a second to respond. "I'm sorry, Mary and Aal are both traveling. Unfortunately I am the one left in charge today. Is there anything I can help you with?"

"I see, well, this is kind of an emergency. I don't know what to do with this little fellow. Can I leave him here with you?"

Darkhorse looked down as the beaver unfolded a soiled, spotted handkerchief.

"What is that?"

"It is a little dead mouse."

"Are you sure it's not a hair clog from a drain?"

The beaver lifted it up by the tail. "See?" Then he placed it back down in the cloth. The little mouse lay unconscious in the small hands of the beaver, and then just barely opened an eye before it shut again.

Darkhorse felt a deep sense of pity for it. No creature deserved to suffer.

"Of course, we will take him and keep him as comfortable as we can until Mary returns."

The sound of the doe's tiny hooves awkwardly descending the stairs sideways grew louder as she approached the landing.

"What's up?" she asked.

"We have a new resident, Fawn. Can I place him on your soft shoulders?" asked Darkhorse.

Fawn grimaced at the sight of what she thought was a ball of mud and hair, but once she recognized that it was a pathetic little creature, her demeanor turned to compassion in an instant. "Oh my gosh, of course," she said softly and turned sideways.

Darkhorse used the tip of his firm hoof to part a small section on Fawn's shoulder fur, and there the beaver gently nestled the tiny cold mouse lying on the handkerchief so it could sink into her warm soft down.

The beaver thanked them and excused himself before he ambled down the stoop, headed straight toward the canal, and dove in to swim home to *Westerkerk*.

IT WAS SOON apparent that the tiny mouse they had rescued was in one of the worst conditions the house has ever hosted. They washed him in a warm bowl of mild detergent and dried him in a fluffy clean washcloth. The other mice helped bundle him up and took care of him, setting him into one of the tiny chairs by the fire next to the frozen pet birds. For hours, the little mouse shivered, speechless, and then fell asleep. Soon, he was able to hold his head up on his own.

After a few hours, he could chew and swallow, so they fed

him warm broth, then tea and honey, and soon the little mouse was able to gnaw on morsels of barley toast.

Despite the kind assurances of the others, he remained silent, morosely staring longingly at the fireplace. Mary would have her work cut out for her with this one.

21

M ary left Edinburgh feeling triumphant. The shadow of Tycho and her bike danced over roofs, treetops and prairies as they coasted above the small suburbs of North Holland toward home. After crossing the large bay known as Amsterdam North's IJ, they crossed Central Station with the large capital letters *AMSTERDAM* on the roof and proceeded on toward the canal district. The long shadowy shapes of living realm tour boats slid under bridges as they soared past the familiar towers of *Norderkerk* (North Church), then *Westerkerk*.

Gliding along *Herengracht*, they descended between the trees and the houses over the road below. Mary spotted Dark-horse and Aal sitting together on the concrete edge of the canal in front of the house, enjoying the sun and the late morning air. The bike's rubber tires, touched down onto the red brick and coasted toward them. She greeted her beloved friends, who received her warmly and she parked her bike between the silver steel tubes near the edge of the canal.

Tycho eagerly fished out a plastic take-away bag from the bike's basket and fluttered in front of Darkhorse's eyeline.

Darkhorse sat up as the warm, aromatic bag of spicy food

bobbed before him. "Is this... veggie vindaloo from Edinburgh? No way! Thank you, Tycho!"

Tycho squeaked, squinting a smile, and perched gently upon Darkhorse's left shoulder, helped untie the bag, and attached chopsticks to his hooves.

"Aal, what are you doing back?" Mary asked.

"I discovered time portal in the Mayan Riviera and I was able to compact three weeks of travel into what for you were just two days, it was a marvelous use of time and magic. I visited many old friends and made new ones as well."

"Wauw!" Mary exclaimed.

"Before departing I found Luis, your bartender friend from the train in Frankfurt, and I healed him in a jiffy. After healing that terrible cough, we became fast friends and I invited him to accompany me to Lourdes for replenishment. We had such a good time, that he joined my entourage on our scheduled Grand Tour. Luis was due for a holiday anyway and he insisted on a trip to his home town. We set out exploring deep into Central America, the Amazon, then the Outback, and the Yukon. So much to tell, but enough about that. Did anything happen here while I was gone?" he smiled coyly.

"Surely you heard I dispatched the Soul Reaper," Mary replied.

"Yes, I did hear something about that. An eruption in the red-light district that was felt even in the living realm. Sounds like you had a *blast*."

Darkhorse moaned at the pun with a mouthful of vindaloo.

Aal smiled knowingly. "But your trip to the council went well?"

"Yes, it went very well, but I am still a bit overwhelmed."

"We took quite the tour of Scotland, even ventured north-west all the way to Islay," Tycho said.

"Islay you say?" the eel could hardly contain himself, knowing that Mary would never return from the island famous for its world-class distilleries without a bottle of finely crafted malt treat.

"I found this for you," she said and placed a charmingly crude, hand-labeled jar of finely aged, cask-strength whisky into the clasp of his tiny fins.

He set it down on the cement and proceeded to wrap half his torso around it. His keen senses relished the smoky character and the earthy peat through the glass. He cooed with delight. "Mary, you truly never disappoint."

Darkhorse sent chunks of vindaloo and rice flying out of his mouth when he burst out as he remembered. "Oh Mary, we have a new Tragically Dead member: a mouse. He was dropped off this morning, no history and no case file." He chewed and took a breath. "He is in rough shape."

"Oh, all right. I think I'll get on it then. Aal, we must catch up later."

"Of course, my dear Mary," the eel replied.

WHEN SHE ENTERED the main room, she was warmly greeted by the rest of the house. Mary quickly gave her attention to the newest resident resting on the mantel. She approached and knelt to get a closer look at the little mouse. He opened his eyes and seemed delighted by Mary.

"Hello, I am Mary van Amsterdam. What are you called?"

He stood up from of his tiny chair, turned, and silently looked up at her through tears. Trembling intermittently, he'd not completely recovered from the cold and trauma.

Mary said, "Well, I am eager to learn more about you. Would it be all right with you if we had some hot tea and got to know one another?"

The mouse nodded in response to Mary's invitation. Even without a file, she could proceed with recovery, orienting the little soul to the afterlife while conducting an introductory assessment. She carried the little mouse up to her consultation space in the attic suite, interested to learn his story.

She placed the mouse on a pillow on the chair across from her and spoke softly. "I am Mary. What would you like to be called?"

The sickly rodent gingerly avoided the subject. Instead he asked her, "How long have you been here?"

"I have been here for more than seventy living-realm years. Do you know how long you have been here?"

Mary then asked him another series of simple questions, but nevertheless the little mouse could only weep softly. She sensed in the mouse feelings of mixed emotions: sadness and joy, but also great yearning, shame and pain. It had been through something terrible. She just needed to find out what it was in order to help him.

The mouse looked uncomfortable in his little rotund body as if it was foreign to him. Mary opened a chest that held several pillows of various sizes and retrieved a velvety one featuring a small pocket, the perfect size for him. She placed it on the chair, leaned back against the backrest, and gently helped the little mouse into place. Mary expected that the pocket would be warm and comfortable for him.

"There you are, darling," Mary said.

The mouse settled in and smiled across from her.

"I can sense that you have been through a terrible trauma. What can you tell me? Start wherever you want."

The tiny mouse looked down for a few seconds, looking as if he was struggling to form the right words. "Well, I awoke in Amsterdam, cold and frightened, terrified and lonely. I don't even speak Dutch. I nearly drowned. I was always scavenging for food. I couldn't recognize how to get around, so I spent a lot of time wandering, wondering where I was. I was lost every day, until eventually I swam to the church, but I couldn't find a way to get out of the canal. I was scared and wet and forced to swim." He stopped and looked up at her. His eyes began to well up again, but Mary encouraged him to keep talking.

"Tell me, do you remember your death?"

"I didn't die."

"You wouldn't be in the afterlife if you didn't die."

"No, I have never died. Before this, I was a monster."

"What kind of monster?"

"A Soul Reaper."

Mary was stunned. "Were you the Soul Reaper that I...?"

"Attacked in the alley, yes."

"No, you can't be. Are you sure?"

"You had to protect your friends, so you made me into this meek little mouse."

Mary gripped her pendant charm. "Well, now that you seem to be able to speak, explain yourself, Soul Reaper. You sent the bartender from the train into a horrific state of Death Cough, and nearly got me twice. You continually attacked me and my friends. Why?"

The little mouse cried, "I never intended to hurt you or your friends. I couldn't control the Soul Reaper body. I am only human. I went through hell trying to get back to you, Mary. I love you!"

Mary now had a stalker. She had dealt with dead who had similarly unhealthy infatuations before, but this was different. "Back to me? Who are you?"

The little mouse hopped out of the pocket and stood there on the table before her, crying. It then occurred to her that rather than ask it, her pendant could show her everything. She had to know what was going on. What was the true nature of this entity? With one hand, she clasped the charmed pendant, and with the other she gently held the hand of the little mouse. Her eyes turned flat white and she commanded the elements, "Reveal to me, who is the essence of the hand I am holding?"

Swirls of light and energy emitted from both Mary and the mouse. As a glowing maelstrom grew, she saw him.

A young man with sandy brown hair was standing across from her. "I am Peter."

"Peter?" she said, trying to grasp the situation.

"Peter, from the attic, remember we'd looked out at the chestnut tree? Mary, I've been so desperate to find you in the afterlife," he said.

"No! Peter?!" Mary yelped, absolutely overtaken by emotion at the reunion.

The swirling field of light turned amber, and Mary transformed into her appearance in the living realm. They stood there in an attic suite annex, embracing again, the innocent teenagers they once were, brave and defiant refugees in hiding once trapped in a very different Amsterdam. They held each other sobbing like roaring lions.

This was too much to believe, let alone understand.

A determined hoof clopped loudly on the wooden door. Darkhorse shouted, "Hey, what's going on in there?"

Mary wiped her tears and with a cracking voice said, "Darkhorse, everything is fine."

She held Peter at arm's length to look over her old friend. It was him. Hard to believe, but it was him. Darkhorse opened the door and glared at what he saw – a young man embracing Mary.

"Darkhorse, this is my old, dear friend Peter. He was..."

The door slammed, and Darkhorse hurriedly descended the stairs. In a matter of seconds, Peter's temporary form as a young man reverted into the mouse he was in the afterlife.

"So, you weren't trying to harm us?" asked Mary.

"Of course I wasn't."

Aal and Tycho came up to see what Darkhorse had described as "some guy hugging Mary," but all they saw was Mary holding a mouse.

. . .

MARY EVENTUALLY CAME OUTSIDE to the canal's edge and found Darkhorse brooding.

"Who is that guy?"

"It is an old friend, someone I know from mu time in the living realm."

"Are you still going to make time for us?"

"Of course, the Tragically Dead are my main priority and always will be. You have to understand that when you encounter someone who you haven't seen for so long—someone who crossed realms to find you, it is a bit overwhelming. But nothing will keep me from my dedication to helping you find peace here.

"Does he know that?"

"I will tell him."

"What if he doesn't like it?"

"Well, tough cheese. No one can keep me from my devotion to you all. The trip to Edinburgh really has reinforced for me, that I am doing the right things here. This is what I died for."

After some time, Mary convinced Darkhorse to join her, Aal, Tycho and Peter on the roof.

That evening, on the rooftop, Peter told of his harrowing journey to the afterlife. The harrowing events that led to his hijacking the body of a Soul Reaper.

"But Mary didn't know you were her friend? You kept attacking us." Darkhorse said. "Why didn't Mary's defensive spells kill Peter instead of turning him into a mouse?"

They sat in silence for a moment, then Aal said, "Mary's abilities are all meant to protect her friends. Even if she didn't know it was Peter, her magic did, so it didn't kill him. He was her friend after all, so the spell simply turned him into a lesser threat – an unconscious mouse."

"I've been here for so long, but there is still much to be learned from the afterlife," Mary said.

"Indeed," Aal replied, "There will clearly be much more in store for everyone."

The group chatted and shared each ones unique stories of life and death. Eventually they toasted before the orange glow of the sunset, to their sometimes messy but never dull union as the Tragically Dead in Recovery.

MARY VAN AMSTERDAM AND THE RESISTANCE OF THE NEW DAWN | AMSTERDAM AFTERLIFE SERIES: BOOK 2, CHAPTER 1

Under the shade of vendor canopies, Mary traded one ice-cream token (the unofficial currency of the afterlife) for a hefty paper bag of Turkish figs. Her eyes smiled as she thanked the charming gray weasel-spirit. Propped high on a stool, he grinned and winked. Mary noticed he had a familiar old-fashioned pocket-watch chain draping from the pocket of his tweed waistcoat.

Amsterdam Afterlife Series: Book Two

"Pardon me. Do you have the time?" Mary asked. The weasel quickly fished out the timepiece and flipped it open, "It's fifteen minutes to eleven, Mary."

"That's a beautiful watch."

"Thank you, this was a gift from a dear friend. It requires some maintenance, but I enjoy it. Never had the capacity to use one properly in the living realm."

"Remind me of your name?" she asked politely.

"Oh, we haven't met Mary. I am Gorik. I'm a great admirer of your work with the Tragically Dead. I see you all have invaded the market today," he said, smiling.

"Yes, we are preparing a little celebration for a recent addition to the house."

"A fresh arrival? What species? Was it one of the wild ones we've heard about?"

"Well, the answer is complicated. For now, he is a mouse."

The weasel cocked his head sideways. "I hope you know we all approve of your handling of the Soul Reaper," with a raised paw, the weasel pointed, "he had what was coming if you ask me. Thank you for all your work for the Amsterdam Afterlife and those sweet souls, Mary. Any of us could have arrived here, confused and injured."

"Thank you for your words of encouragement." Mary smiled and departed the shade of the vendor canopy.

She searched the stalls of the market for a gift for Peter. A pocket-watch, like that, would be perfect. That was it! She recalled that during their childhood, Peter had possession of one. Their existence under siege was full of uncertainty, and such belongings were rare and cherished. Still, eventually it had to be traded to pay the people who hid them during the wartime activity of Amsterdam.

Inspired by this recovered memory, Mary headed toward a vendor selling such things. One of her many housemates, a feisty little doe called Fawn, caught up to her.

"Did you find anything for Peter yet?"

"No, but I think I know just the thing."

"Where are you headed?"

"I'm going right over there, where the jewelry vendors usually set-up."

"Jewelry, are you getting a *ring*? Are you and little Peter going to get *married*?" she teased in her high-pitched voice.

"No, I am certain that is not happening," Mary said uncomfortably as she glanced about to ensure Darkhorse wasn't close enough to catch a whisper of the notion. As she approached the jewelry seller, Mary was disappointed to remember Peter was no longer a young man, but a tiny little mouse. He wouldn't be able to do anything useful with a human-sized pocket watch. It was bigger than he was. Should she give it to him as a symbol, promising to find a way to transform him back into a human? Or would such a gift give him false hope? She wasn't confident she could acquire such magic. As the friction of the problem ground her mind down, the pace of her walk slowed until she stood in place, defeated. The little doe brushed past Mary, making a beeline for the display case.

Fawn enjoyed haggling and took it upon herself to question the legitimacy of wares offered by the vendor. The Amsterdam hucksters were the few on the afterlife continent, well-matched for her.

Fawn raised her tiny hoof toward what appeared to be an

excellent collection of luxury watches behind scratched display glass. Tapping her cloven foot on the case, she asked incredulously, "Are these even real?"

The seller was an unshaven man eating a sandwich. He turned around and said in a gravelly voice, with a mouth full of food, "You can see them, you can touch them. They're real!"

He grinned with crumbs and mustard dripping down his chin and glanced over to a fellow huckster, an emu reading a newspaper in the adjacent stall. They both let out hearty chuckles, and the man set his food down. He wiped off his thick fingers with a napkin and leaned down on the glass toward Fawn, sucking his teeth.

"Look, little one, for fifty ice-cream tokens, you can take your pick. It's a good price, you know?"

She turned her head sideways and stared at him with narrowed eyes.

"Really?"

He held his hands up and said, "Trust me, Bambi, you can't get a better price on these anywhere else."

Mary knew Fawn hated the comparison but hoped she would restrain herself from one of her furious tantrums, potentially ending with piercing blows from her sharp, cloven hooves. Fawn stared at the man for several seconds before Mary glided over, placing herself between the doe and the glass case.

"Thank you, sir," she said, and with a glow from her pendant, created a magical push gently propelling the little doe around. "All right, let's move on." Fawn reluctantly trotted away with Mary as the vendor continued his pitch—now to both.

"Hey, Mary van Amsterdam! You deserve some new jewelry —always wearing that same necklace!"

Mary ignored him and nudged Fawn to keep moving along.

"Giving them the third-degree?" She asked.

"These vendors would steal from their own mothers, I tell ya!" she said.

Mary chuckled. "Some of them, perhaps."

With no official currency, purchases, even exchanges just for ice-cream tokens were more akin to bartering. Such transactions fell under the category of *buyer beware*, but in general, the afterlife was a safe place, full of trustworthy spirits.

"Fawn, I need your help."

"You still haven't found anything for Peter?"

"Not yet," Mary said as she desperately surveyed the stalls, "not yet."

"Do you think you can help turn him back into a human?"

"I will consult further with Aal, I'm sure there is a way."

"Hey, Mary, maybe we should try *Waterlooplein*?"

"Well, I'm afraid we don't have time, Fawn."

"But it's on the way, and I want to see if my friend Zono is there. Besides, they have fresh-pressed stroopwafels."

As the doe continued arguing her case for hitting up *Waterlooplein* on the route home, Mary spied her Tragically Dead friends, Darkhorse and the raven, Tycho, at a nearby stall. She was proud of the handsome corvid with his charmed golden beak. His adaption to the Amsterdam Afterlife was remarkable. She wished Peter could get along so well among the group. The sight of Tycho perched upon the grim shoulder of the dead horse made her smile.

The two spirits were sorting through a series of bins packed with dusty archives of comic books, CDs, and vinyl. In the past decade, such artifacts of underground culture had become Darkhorse's newfound passion. Much taller than the average human, his black-cloaked equine skeleton hunched over to view the items. Alone, he would have struggled to sort through the bins with his massive hooves, but Tycho's beak and claws aided his search for media gold.

Mary opened the paper bag of figs.

"Care for a fig?" she asked Fawn as she gazed in appreciation of her friends' conviviality.

"Figs? Nah, I want to save my appetite for the stroop—"

"Have a fig." Mary hushed her by shoving a whole dried fruit in the doe's mouth.

The doe muttered something unintelligible while chewing the massive plummy sweet. Mary approached discretely, hoping to observe the budding friendship of the raven and horse spirits. Historically, Darkhorse had a difficult time making friends. He was moody and had a habit of inadvertently pushing others away, but she hoped this special friendship would be different.

With his dexterous claws and beak Tycho generously revealed each item of the bins with excellent efficiency. The rare and imported titles of most interest to Darkhorse would be easy to recognize but hard to come by.

"Nothing," Darkhorse moaned in his deep voice as they completed scouring a bin. They moved on to the next row of media. The raven quickly flipped through for Darkhorse to scan.

"Should we get something for Peter?" Tycho asked Darkhorse.

"Meh. I'm not getting anything. That's Mary's problem, he's her friend."

"Oh. I see," the innocent raven said.

"All right, maybe this is something. I never thought I'd see this one in the afterlife." Darkhorse examined the back of an LP.

"You don't like him, do you?" asked the raven.

"Peter? I dunno. You do recall he was the Soul Reaper who tried to kill us before Mary turned him into a mouse?" said Darkhorse.

"Yeah, but we now know he wasn't trying to kill us. He was

just trying to get Mary's attention. He claims it was hard to control the body of the Soul Reaper. We can't hold what he did against him. He deserves the benefit of the doubt. Besides," Tycho's voice grew wistful as he continued, "think how amazing it is that he crossed dimensions to reunite with his true love, Mary." The raven stared up at the sky wistfully. "As Aal says, it's romantic."

"Yuck," Darkhorse replied and resumed sorting through the stacks of vinyl.

Mary looked solemn as she heard the conversation unfold, standing covertly around the corner. Both she and the Fawn were still unseen by Tycho and Darkhorse. She had barely managed to chew her fig but had done so enough to prepare to say something snarky and reveal their presence. Fawn held up her cloven hoof, but before the doe could speak, Mary clasped her charmed pendant, and the two disappeared into the ether for a moment. They reappeared several meters away, leaving only a thin wisp of blue smoke at their original location.

"Don't tell them we were spying," Mary insisted.

The doe murmured, her mouth still full of fig.

Mary persisted elsewhere to find something for Peter, lost in her own thoughts. Fawn regained her bearings and trotted off in the direction of Darkhorse and Tycho.

The doe pushed through Darkhorse's cloak, passed between his legs, and her cold snout poked up at one of the records under his hoof. She swallowed enough to exclaim, "Oh, Abba!" Chunks of half-chewed fig spattered onto the plastic sleeve of the album Tycho was holding to the side, as they searched for something more up Darkhorse's alley.

"Sheesh, Fawn, you almost gave me a heart attack," Darkhorse said, startled.

The raven gently brushed the pieces off the surface with his bluish-black wing.

"That's impossible, you don't have a heart," she replied.

"I'd appreciate it if you didn't bring up the inadequacies of my grim corporeal representation, thank you!" Darkhorse said.

"Sorry," she replied, with a subtle tinge of sarcasm. "I don't even know what you just said, but Mary says she wants to go to *Waterlooplein* next."

"Ok, cool, they have a great stroopwafel stand there, Tycho."

"I've never tried them," the raven replied.

"We'll follow you," Darkhorse said to Fawn.

BEHIND THE ROWS of market vendors, the ominous sixteenth-century structure, the Waag loomed over the square—replete with thick medieval turrets. During medieval times, it was the city gate, the last remnant of the old wall around Amsterdam. Mary strode briskly under its shadow.

Fawn caught up to her and asked, "Why'd you run off?"

Mary said, "It was unsettling to hear Darkhorse's feelings about Peter. It felt wrong to spy."

"Whatever, there was nothing you didn't already know, right? So, what are you getting for Peter?"

"I truly have no idea."

Mary and Peter were very different people than when they

were living children. She no longer shared his sustained enthusiasm for their reunion. After just a few days, all the feelings that caused her to end their relationship in the living realm seem to have returned tenfold.

"Yeah. 'What to buy your boyfriend, who crossed over to join you in the afterlife in the form a Soul Reaper and tried to kill you?'" Fawn said, "Sounds like a blurb right off the cover of a Cosmo."

Mary laughed for the first time since Peter arrived, then added, "And who, you then, accidentally transformed into a mouse?"

"Yeah," Fawn chuckled, "You are a one of a kind, Mary, that's why we love you."

Mary let Fawn lead the group out of New Market and marched south, past Rembrandt's House. By the time she realized Fawn wasn't taking them home, but to the market at *Waterlooplein*, she had warmed to the idea and didn't rebuke the doe's persistence. The Tragically Dead deserved a treat, and perhaps she could find a gift for Peter there.

Out of a dim, narrow alleyway, they emerged into this second market square of the day. At one stall with old books and magazines, Mary found an old stack of photos. The images from the 1930s and 40s instantly brought up nostalgia for her former life in the living realm of Amsterdam. A tin box caught her attention, and in it, she discovered a waxy paper envelope containing photos from the Jordaan district. Finally, something related to a memory she and Peter shared! It was a small, well-worn, but charming set of images of the old borough. One depicting *Westerkerk* caught her eye.

The print was in good shape, perhaps cut from the back of a large box of matches or out of a pamphlet and appeared to have been lovingly hand-tinted. The globe atop the tower was still gold, just as it was when Mary and Peter used to gaze upon it through the window of the attic. After the war, it returned to a blue color. Transfixed, Mary felt a rush of memories. The card was at least a hundred-years-old and had a nostalgic aura she hoped would speak to Peter as much as it did to her.

She procured the antique image along with a few colorful stickers she thought Fawn might like, in exchange for a single ice-cream token. She had completed her goal and combed the rows of vendors, gathering the other Tragically Dead.

AFTER A SHORT TIME, Mary led them out of the square. The group was indulging in warm stroopwafels as they approached *Blauwbrug*. But when they got to the bridge, something there wasn't right. A crowd was blocking the way across. Their attention appeared to be focused on a stalled tram.

"Was someone struck?" Mary asked a dead heron.

"I don't know," he said, then looked back and saw Mary's Tragically Dead standing behind her.

"Oh, Mary! Well, I can tell you there is certainly no tram stop on the span. You must do something about these feral arrivals! Why do we keep getting souls from the afterlife who act so unruly?"

"We are doing our best to find out," Mary said apologetically, "It's important to treat each individual with dignity and understanding. No one ever comes to the Afterlife with evil as their intention."

"I know you are doing your best as our guardian, but these incidents are now almost a daily occurrence," the heron said.

From behind the tram, loud unsettling growls rang out. With a chorus of screams, a group of panicking dead residents poured around the edge of the cars, rushing in desperate efforts to flee the unseen event on the other side.

Shadow forms of startled living souls, too, fled the scene. Several ran straight through Mary and the other spirits standing there. Something terrible and possibly trans-dimensional was occurring.

As they got closer, they saw a crowd giving a wide berth to what remained out of sight, behind the tram. Mary rushed to the other side of the bridge to see around the tramcar. There she saw an enormous wild wolf. It stood menacingly on its hind legs, in a daze—growling and snarling fiercely as it surveyed the surrounding intermingled crowd, from both the living realm and the afterlife, blocking the tracks. Taller than Darkhorse, the lupine form was massive with huge clawed paws planted on the stone. Mary noticed one hind leg had a living realm trap clamped tightly. Surrounding the steel teeth of the swollen injury, blood had dried into the matted down fur.

The wolf staggered toward the pavement section of the span, swiping at a group of innocents attempting to pass. An emu spirit panicked and leaped from the edge of the bridge in terror into the river Amstel. With the wolf off the tracks, the tram powered up with haste to continue. Overhead, electric cables cracked and buzzed as the crowd parted and its driver got away.

Now the wolf-spirit was in full view on the bridge. Bicyclists passed around the drooling creature in haste. The situation was terrifying.

"Here's an idea, let's go back and head up Singel instead, eh?" said Fawn swiftly.

"I have to go talk to her," Mary said without hesitation. She placed her bags on Darkhorse's extended left hoof, gripped her magical pendant, levitated off the ground, and swiftly glided through the crowd to reach the vicious wolf.

"Here we go again," moaned Darkhorse.

Tycho gracefully launched off Darkhorse, following Mary through the air, and landed gently on her shoulder. She stood just a few meters away from the wolf. "Hello, I am Mary. What's your name?"

The wolf turned and growled at her. Appearing uninterested in pleasantries, it stalked toward her, limping, and sneered with clinched teeth inches from her face. It looked like the massive beast could take off her head in one chomp. Fearlessly, Mary held her ground. She looked deeply into the eyes of the drooling wolf with compassion. A mystical emanation grew from the pendant she gripped, transmitting genuine benevolent intention and empathy for the wolf.

The beast raised its enormous front paw, claws extended. It looked as if it would take a swipe at her. Fawn let out an expletive. Darkhorse covered his eyes with his hooves. Tycho gripped the shoulder of Mary's dress, ready to whisk her off to safety. But time seemed to slow as waves of energy grew like rings in a still pond from Mary's chest. The tension among every spirit on the bridge melted as Mary's afterlife gift enabled a transformative encounter. Mesmerized by Mary's radiating empathy and bravery, the wolf retracted her claws and lowered her front paw. Like an obedient dog, she closed her mouth and sat down gently before Mary. Even seated, the wolf was taller than her. Mary correctly oriented the beast, providing conditioning she should have received naturally before arriving in the Amsterdam Afterlife. As the effects of the re-orientation set in, the wolf's posture relaxed. As if she was coming out of a trance, she cocked her head, peering at Mary like a curious dog and uttered, "I am Kiza, I am in search of my young, do you know where they have taken my pups?"

"I don't know, Kiza, but I will help you. Your pups' well-being is important. I will do all I can to help you if you let me."

A dead woman in a wide-brimmed hat arrived on her bike. At a safe distance from the encounter, she pointed to Mary standing before Kiza, she yelled out, "Another wild beast has arrived in the afterlife! That thing is dangerous, why are you helping it? It doesn't belong here!"

"Take it easy, lady, this is Mary van Amsterdam, ever heard of her? The guardian of the afterlife?" Fawn's chiding embarrassed the woman. She promptly turned her nose to the air, got on her bike, and rode away, pursing her lips.

Mary and the wolf had calmly locked eyes upon one another, establishing an unspoken understanding.

"Kiza, I can remove this trap from your leg."

The wolf looked down at the trap clamping relentlessly on her but said nothing.

"Would that be all right? I think you will feel much better if you allow me to remove it."

The wolf blinked, then said, "Yes, please."

"Tycho, please go fetch my purse from Darkhorse," Mary whispered, maintaining eye-contact with Kiza.

Mary clasped her pendant, and the mouth of the animal trap creaked opened. Its sharp teeth parted to reveal deep, painful-looking gashes in the wolf's boney ankle. As Mary's willed it, the device floated off from the leg and dropped onto the pavement. Tycho arrived and handed Mary's purse over.

"Tycho, please take our new friend's trap over by the garbage bin, so it doesn't block the bridge."

The raven effortlessly took the chain from the steel device into his enchanted beak. Thanks to its magic, he delivered the heavy steel trap onto the bank of the canal. Blood gushed out of the wound, and the wolf doubled over pressing her leg.

Mary reached into her bag and retrieved a vial of potion. She soaked a cotton cloth with its entire contents and knelt before the wolf. Simultaneously holding her pendant, Mary applied the serum. In seconds it erased all Kiza's physical discomfort and transformed the wound into a furless scar.

Although the physical pain from the injury dissipated, nothing could so quickly ease the anguish of her separation from her pups. With words of wisdom, Mary calmed the mother-wolf and invited her to join her on the walk home.

After a few more moments talking, Mary glanced over her shoulder to Darkhorse and the others signaling for them to follow. Mary and Kiza departed the bridge together, chatting softly, and the crowd of onlookers dispersed.

"So, should we follow them?" asked the doe.

"Yeah, let's give them privacy, though," said Darkhorse.

Tycho returned to Darkhorse's shoulder.

"We healed her," the raven replied as they walked. "The wolf is a mother who is upset because she can't find her cubs. I don't think she knew she was dead."

"Mary does this—it's who she is," said Darkhorse, "She somehow manages to see the good in everyone."

. . .

CONTINUE the journey as Mary confronts the rise of "The New Dawn"...

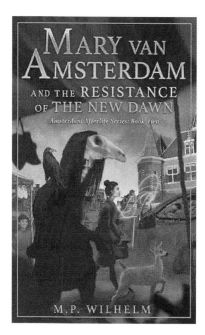

Amsterdam Afterlife Series: Book Two

STAY IN TOUCH WITH THE AMSTERDAM AFTERLIFE

For more content, illustrations and information on new releases from the Amsterdam Afterlife visit www.MaryVanAmsterdam.com

If you enjoyed this book, please leave a review on the product page and better yet, share the book with a friend!

facebook.com/maryvanamsterdam

twitter.com/maryvanamsterd1

instagram.com/maryvanamsterdam

amazon.com/M.-P.-Wilhelm

pinterest.com/marvyvanamsterdam

goodreads.com/marcwilhelm

youtube.com/maryvanamsterdam

Get the FREE short story prequel for signing up for Amsterdam Afterlife updates at maryvanamsterdam.com

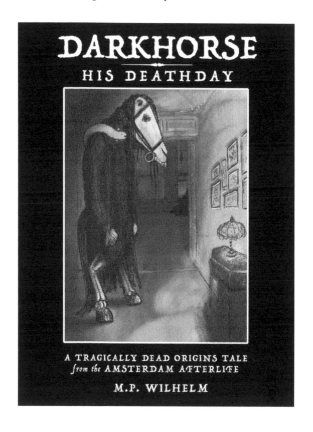

Amsterdam Afterlife: Book Three (Late Spring, 2020)

ABOUT THE AUTHOR

M. P. Wilhelm was born and raised in Colorado. For two decades, his career as a professional game designer led to the development of iconic game franchises and an appointment as a professor in a top-ranked game design program.

Creating art and experiences, with or without a controller, has always been his passion. Two years living in the canal district of Amsterdam, Holland, inspired him to create the Amsterdam Afterlife, Mary van Amsterdam and the Tragically Dead in Recovery.

When not writing or illustrating, he loves to study history, travel, read, and play. Under the shadow of Colorado's Rocky Mountains, he hikes each day with his ridiculously adorable dog, Bravo.

Made in the USA
Monee, IL
03 March 2020

22662066R00122